The Doomsday Device (The Teen Superheroes Series)

Copyright 2012 Darrell Pitt

Find out more about Darrell at his website:

http://www.darrellpitt.com

Email: darrellpitt@gmail.com

Dedicated to:
Robert Arthur

Teen Superheroes

Book Two

The Doomsday Device

Prolog

My name is Axel.

No last name. No middle name. Just Axel.

If people ask me my surname I tell them it's Smith. I know that's not terribly original, but it sounds so phony people never guess it really is fictitious. There's a good reason why I don't have a last name and here it is.

Okay. Deep breath.

I was part of a secret experiment carried out by an organization known as The Agency. This organization works in conjunction with an alien race known as The Bakari. They've been here on Earth for thousands of years. The experiment was known as Project Alpha and their goal was to create superheroes.

Why? The Bakari don't want to interfere in human affairs, but neither do they want to see us destroy ourselves. One day the human race will join the intergalactic club. They're still waiting for us to evolve enough as a species for that day to arrive.

During the process my memory was wiped and I was given amazing powers. I can manipulate air. I can compress it and turn it into a shield or a weapon. I can shape it into an invisible glider on which I can fly or I can create a vacuum leaving someone else struggling for breath.

So don't make me mad.

And here's the rest of it. I'm seventeen (I think—it's hard to know when you have no memory) with brown hair, brown eyes and a small scar on the left side of my chin. I'm a native of the old US of A, but don't ask me which part because I don't know.

My looks won't put me on the front cover of any magazines, but I'm also not ugly either.

Oh, and I'm not alone. There's Chad. He's about the same age, but he's from Norway. He can create fire and ice. Also, he's a pain (more on that later).

His sister Ebony looks about the same age. Like her brother, she has blonde hair and blue eyes. She is attractive and can transmute objects to any substance she wants. That's handy if you want to turn coal into diamonds and you don't have twenty million years to spare.

Next on the list is Brodie. She's an Australian with red hair and a pretty face. She's my girlfriend. Kind of. In a way.

Confused?

Not half as much as me.

Then there's Dan. He's a couple of years younger. Probably about fourteen. He's Chinese, but he speaks perfect English. He can manipulate metals with his mind. He can also pick up on the emotional states of the other members of our group. So if one of us is in pain—he's the first to know. He can also manipulate people's minds too. If you were playing poker against him you would probably want to double check your cards. Maybe those aren't three six's you're carrying.

They could be aces.

And then there's Ferdy. How would I start to describe Ferdy? Let's see. He's a little younger like Dan. He has a brain like a computer. He can remember amazing facts and do incredible calculations in his head. We're pretty sure he's autistic because he doesn't seem to be able to communicate with the rest of us. He spends a lot of time in his own world, so we do our best to draw him out as part of the gang.

Oh, I forgot something.

He has super strength and can lift up a bus.

So don't make him mad either.

And that's us. We're teenage superheroes, but right now we're trying to lay low and get our lives back together. The Agency gave us a campervan (actually we stole it from them) and we're renting a house outside Las Vegas. The Agency allowed us to go, but we agreed they could call on us for help if required.

The people at The Agency are not our friends, but we hope they're not our enemies either. If they leave us alone we'll do the same.

So, that's us.

Chapter One

Everything was fine until someone decided to blow up the plane.

I was sitting toward the rear. One of those air crash investigation programs said that passengers sitting toward the rear have a better chance of surviving an air crash. Call me afraid. Call me a coward. Call me whatever you want. So what if I have super powers? It doesn't mean I'm invincible.

We were returning from Dallas on yet another one of our trips to discover our origins. When we left The Agency we took with us an encrypted book containing lists of addresses from across the planet. So far we had visited about twenty of them expecting to discover that we had lived at one of these premises.

So far we had turned up exactly—nothing.

Some of the addresses were residential homes. Others were businesses. A couple were factories. We could find no link between us and the addresses.

We had not given up hope, but we were discouraged. One of the scientists at The Agency—

Doctor Sokolov—had told me some crucial information with her dying breath. She had told me I had a brother.

Somewhere out there I had a family member. All I had to do was find him.

I let out a deep sigh and glanced around the interior of the plane. Dan was seated next to the window. We had taken a lot of flights over the last six months—ever since we had acquired our super powers—and he always grabbed the window seat. Watching the world fly by held no great allure for me.

I had done plenty of flying.

Most of it without an airplane.

The jet was traveling from Dallas to Las Vegas. I was sitting next to Dan. Brodie, Ebony and Chad were toward the front adjacent to the wings. It was a typical flight. Flying in a plane is actually quite boring when you've flown without one. I had watched most of the in-flight movie. Then I'd moved onto a book. Finally I had tried closing my eyes to grab forty winks.

I opened my eyes and glanced at my watch.

Thirty minutes till we were due to land.

Not my idea of fun.

Dan sat forward and rubbed his forehead.

'Everything okay?' I asked.

He did not immediately reply. Finally he said, 'Yeah.'

He didn't sound all right.

'I've got one of those headaches,' he said.

I knew what he meant by those headaches.

The Alpha Project had left Dan with an odd set of abilities. He was able to control metal objects. He could also manipulate people's minds like in Star Wars. You know, like those old Jedi mind tricks. In addition he could pick up the feelings and thoughts of other people. It had begun with us, but over recent months he had started to hear the thoughts of other people too.

'What can you hear?' I asked him quietly.

He didn't say anything for the longest time. Then he said, 'A guy. He's got...bad thoughts.'

Bad thoughts. That could mean anything from being a serial killer to painting graffiti on city buildings.

'He's got...' Dan stopped. 'He's carrying some sort of weapon.'

I looked across the rows of seats before us. This was a 747 carrying a full load of passengers. From memory that numbered around four hundred and fifty passengers. Air marshals were not unusual on flights. Not only were they authorized to carry a weapon, but they were allowed to use them in case of emergencies.

'A bomb,' Dan said quietly.

'Wassat?'

Now Dan had my full attention. He looked up at me with fear in his eyes. 'He's carrying a bomb around his waist. I think he...killed his wife this morning. I can see blood. Lots of it. He's been planning this for ages. This morning...this morning was the trigger.'

A chill choked my spine.

'Who is it?' I asked.

Dan shook his head. 'I have no idea.'

'You've got to focus,' I told him. 'You've

done it before.'

He had done it before. He had picked out the thoughts of a single person who had stolen jewelry from a store. Unfortunately it had taken almost half an hour and left him with a blinding headache.

'I'm not sure—'

'Just try. I'll tell the others.'

I started down the aisle, swerving by children and their parents heading to the restrooms and the attendants trying to force feed the passengers. I could just make out Brodie's red hair. She and Chad were sitting on the window side. Ebony was on the other side of the aisle chatting to Ferdy. She had taken a liking to him and seemed to have made it her personal mission to draw him out of his shell.

I wasn't too sure how much success she was having. Ferdy obviously suffered from some kind of autism, but without professional advice it was hard to work out the best course of action. So far all our knowledge had been gleaned from the internet.

Chad and Brodie's heads were close to each other, so close in fact that I thought, for one horrible split second, that they were kissing.

It was a disconcerting thought.

I needed to speak to them in private, but jumbo jets are not exactly renowned for privacy. Kneeling next to Brodie, I gripped her armrest and bent low.

'Hey guys,' I said. 'We need to talk.'

Brodie turned to me laughing. 'Axel! Chad was just telling me the funniest story.'

'I'm sure. Look, Dan just told me—'

'Why you looking so serious, Leader man?' Chad asked. 'Did you get a boo-boo?'

There are times I really hate Chad. Sometimes I think he was put on this Earth to drive me crazy. Certainly, he is a friend. Absolutely, I am glad he's on our side.

Still, I want to kill him sometimes.

I spoke in a hushed tone. 'Dan thinks someone has a bomb on this plane.'

Well, that sort of information will kill most conversations very quickly.

'What?' The smile fell from Brodie's face.

'Who?'

'He's trying to work that out.'

'What do you suggest?' Chad asked. 'Should we tell the crew?'

I shrugged. 'Tell them what? Dan can read minds? There's a loony about to blow up the plane?'

'What do we know?' Brodie asked.

'It's a man,' I said. 'That's all.'

'That narrows it down to roughly half the passengers,' Brodie said.

'Probably less,' Chad said. 'Children are maybe five or ten percent.'

I nodded.

'We need to conduct our own search,' Brodie suggested. 'See if we can spot him ourselves.'

'He won't exactly be wearing a sign,' Chad said.

'No, but he might be agitated,' Brodie said.

He might be agitated? I knew I certainly was. Glancing behind me, I saw Ebony watching us curiously. I leant close to Brodie.

'Tell Ebony what's happening,' I told her.

'It's probably best to leave Ferdy where he is. I'll see if Dan has any more information.'

I started back to the rear. As I wandered past everyone, I scanned their faces for signs of guilt. Did any of the men look like they had just murdered their wives? One of them was engaged in a furious discussion with his partner. He looked like he wanted to murder his wife. A guy in the middle of a row of seats was staring into space. He was wearing an odd expression.

But how odd, exactly? Did he look psychotic odd?

Then there was the guy sitting next to the window who was nervously wiping his face. Why did he look so nervous?

By the time I reached Dan I felt confused and he looked unwell.

'Any luck?' I asked.

'Not much,' he said. 'I've got a splitting headache and…'

'And what?'

He shook his head. 'I think the guy's carrying

more than a bomb. I think he's also got a gun.'

A gun? How was such a thing possible? Ever since 9/11 security on all domestic flights had been ramped up to the max. How could someone possibly smuggle a gun and a bomb on board a plane?

It was impossible, unless they had some sort of exemption to carry a weapon on board the flight and the only person allowed to do that would be—

'Dan,' I said urgently. 'Could the person be a sky marshal?'

'A sky marshal?'

'Yes. You know. They're a kind of plain clothes police officer allowed to carry weapons on a plane. They're supposed to look after security, but—'

But in this case the man was probably insane.

Dan nodded slowly. 'I think you're right. I'm getting a sense that he always carries a gun. I think he's some kind of cop.'

I glanced over the rows of seats. Ebony and Brodie were working their way up the aisle closest to us, surreptitiously examining the passengers. Chad was combing the other aisle. He was not quite so secretive. Actually he looked like he was seeking a fight.

Well, he often looked like that.

I grabbed Dan's arm. 'Just follow my lead. Try to get into the stewardesses head when I ask about sky marshals.'

'What?'

I dragged him with me. We pushed past a man and his son returning from the restroom and cornered a pretty air stewardess in one of the galley alcoves. She wore a name tag. Her name was Kelly.

'Excuse me, Miss,' I said.

'Yes?'

She looked at us curiously.

'I'm just trying to settle an argument with my friend,' I said hurriedly. 'We were having a conversation about sky marshals.'

I glanced at Dan. He was staring intently at the girl. Slowly, he turned around and looked back toward the rear of the aircraft.

'Yes?' the stewardess asked curiously.

I made up a story about how I thought women

weren't allowed to be sky marshals. The girl assured me the role was not gender specific. I barely heard what she was saying. I was hoping she was doing exactly what I intended; plane crews were always cognizant as to the identities of any passengers carrying guns. In this case it would be the sky marshal.

After a few seconds I nodded, gripped Dan's arm and dragged us away.

'Speak to me,' I said.

'It's him,' Dan said.

A man in a gray business suit had just left his seat and was slowly making his way to the back. I had not noticed him at all when I scanned the passengers. He was simply another ordinary looking individual on the flight. He reached the back restrooms adjacent to the rear door. His eyes settled on my face.

He knew.

It had to be something in my face. Possibly a look of pure, naked fear. Whatever it was, he immediately looked alarmed and reached into his pocket.

Brodie was in the same aisle heading toward him.

'Brodie!' I yelled. 'It's him!'

She spun around at the sound of my voice, followed my outstretched arm with her eyes and started toward the man. He dragged out a gun and pointed it wildly.

He fired.

I saw Brodie's hand move faster than the eye can see. She reached to her right and was spun around one hundred and eighty degrees. She looked like some sort of drunk ballet dancer. Grabbing an armrest for support, I saw her open her clenched fist.

She had caught the bullet.

People started to scream as the man reached into his pocket. I shoved a man out of the way. I needed to create a wall of air as a weapon, but everything was happening so fast. A woman leapt up in front of me. Someone else fell into the aisle as they tried to escape from the chaos.

The man took a step back. The look on his face was one of amazing calm. He actually looked kind of relieved.

That's when he detonated the bomb.

Chapter Two

General Solomon Wolff shaded his eyes as he stepped from the plane onto the boarding ramp and peered across the tarmac. It was a hot day in Dubai, but then this country was known for its heat. Rain at any time was unusual in Dubai and it was common for the average temperature to reach boiling point in August.

As luck would have it, this was August.

Wolff did not let small things like the heat concern him. He was a mercenary and men like him often enjoyed difficulty as much as they did ease. Sometimes he thought he preferred it more. Heat and discomfort kept him on his toes. He had seen too many of his comrades become sedate or relaxed and that was when they made mistakes.

Mistakes in his line of work usually led to death.

He walked down the passenger stairs and spotted a limousine on the tarmac. A man in a headscarf was waiting for him with a sign. Printed across it in white letters was a single word:

Phillips

This was his agreed upon name for this flight, the latest of many names he had used over the years. He nodded to the driver. The man opened the back door and he climbed in. The back of the vehicle was edged in leather and a gold colored metal which he believed probably actually was gold.

The vehicle started and he sat back and relaxed.

They headed toward the middle of the main shopping district in Dubai. This country was a place of extremes. People still rode camels in this country although others just as happily drove vehicles. The predominant religion was the Muslim faith and here women were required to wear the traditional clothing; the abaya, a black ankle length gown that covered the head. At the same time this was a place of immense wealth and money created freedom. The freedom to build, the freedom to control.

One sign of that freedom dominated the landscape directly in front of Wolff. The world's tallest building—the Burj Khalifa—rose directly from the city before him.

Wolff—or Phillips as he was temporarily known—felt a tiny sense of pride that he was about to attend a meeting in this structure. He stifled the emotion. Pride was a weakness and a weakness that could kill. He forced himself to look out impassively at the passing streets.

Soon the vehicle began to draw close to the undercover parking area.

'Excuse me,' Wolff said.

'Yes, sir?'

'I'll walk the last few feet. Thank you.'

The car drew to a halt. The driver opened his door and Wolff stepped out into the terrible heat once more. He looked up at the Burj Khalifa. Truly this was an amazing structure. Not only was it the world's tallest skyscraper, but it also held records for highest restaurant, highest mosque and highest nightclub.

It held the record for the world's second highest swimming pool, but Wolff doubted the building's owners lost little sleep over not securing that particular record.

A man walked from the main reception of the building to meet him. He wore a suit and unlike many of the other people Wolff had seen here, he did not appear to be an Arab. Wolff suspected he was European.

'Mr. Phillips?' the man said.

'Yes?'

'I am Jean-Pierre Bertrand,' he said, shaking hands with Wolff. 'I notice you decided to examine the structure from the outside.'

'It's most impressive,' Wolff replied.

'It is indeed,' Bertrand said. 'Our meeting will take place on the one hundred and thirtieth floor. I think you will find it a most impressive view.'

Wolff nodded. Bertrand led him through the main foyer to one of the elevators. The attendant pushed a button and they ascended the structure at great speed.

That's right, Wolff thought. *This structure also holds the record for the world's fastest elevators.*

Another record broken.

The elevator came to a precise halt. Bertrand led him out into a foyer and they passed two businessmen leaving a meeting. No doubt they were quite reputable. Most of the dealings that took place in this structure were reputable.

Most meetings.

Some like the one he was about to attend could not be termed reputable by any stretch of the imagination. In fact, disreputable would probably be putting it kindly. Wolff was ready to meet with an individual that would make any Interpol or FBI agent's mouth water with anticipation.

Bertrand arrived at a door and knocked on it three times. After a moment, it opened and a servant showed them into the room. It had a spectacular view of the entire Gulf of Oman.

This is where my life has brought me, Wolff thought. *To the top of the world.*

He was aware of the sense of pride he felt, but he allowed himself to revel in it for a few seconds.

'Impressive, is it not?' a voice said from behind.

Wolff turned slowly. The man who had stepped from the room behind him was of average build. He had brown hair and eyes. Possibly about forty years of age. Clean shaven. No distinguishing marks of any noticeable kind.

'I'm sure you know who I am,' the man said.

'I do,' Wolff replied. 'You are Mercer Todd. I believe you currently hold the number three position on the FBI's most wanted list.'

Todd inclined his head. 'A dubious honor. There are sadists and serial killers on that list. I am not that kind of man.' He smiled. 'However, I sometimes make use of the services of men who are.'

Wolff nodded and said nothing.

'Please take a seat,' Todd said. 'Would you like a drink?'

'Just water would be fine.'

The men sat opposite each other. The chairs were positioned in such a way that they still enjoyed a view of the gulf. A glass arrived for Wolff, but he noticed Todd did not partake.

'I understand you are a man who can get

things,' Todd said.

'I have been known to be able to acquire things under the right circumstances,' Wolff confirmed. 'And for the right price.'

Todd named a price. It was a lot of money. It occurred to Wolff that he never would have thought his services could be considered so valuable; one hundred million dollars was a lot of money in anyone's terms. For such a sum this would not be an easy task, but then he was never contacted to carry out easy assignments.

'You've named your price,' Wolff said. 'Perhaps you should name the thing you require and then I can determine if the two are of a commensurate value.'

Todd nodded. 'I need you to kidnap someone for me. A child. A very important child.'

Wolff said nothing. For one hundred million dollars he imagined it must be the child of a president—possibly the American President—or a prime minister. He asked if this was the case.

The man who rated the number three position

on the FBI's most wanted list smiled. It was not a pleasant smile.

'Oh, no,' he said. 'The child is not famous. Not yet. But he will be.'

Todd named the child.

It was not often that Wolff doubted if he could achieve his task, but this was one of those rare times. He sat for a long moment considering the offer. One hundred million dollars was a lot of money, but he knew he would be earning every cent of it. He had not personally met this child, but he had dealt with his friends. It was fair to say they were possibly the most difficult adversaries he had ever faced.

He would need assistance if he was going to make this mission work.

'They are currently living in a group household,' Todd continued. 'They are using the name of Smith.'

Wolff nodded. 'Where?'

'A house outside of Las Vegas.'

Of course, Wolff thought. *More desert.*

Chapter Three

The blast took out the passenger door to the bomber's left as well as the infrastructure to his right; the restroom disintegrated into debris as did three seats. A roaring sound filled the entire compartment as the air was sucked out of the aircraft; a fine mist filled the air. People screamed as oxygen masks fell from the ceiling.

It was mayhem. Absolute mayhem.

The plane lurched to one side. I saw the vacuum of air dragging a man helplessly along the aisle toward the breach in the cabin. Another passenger grabbed hold of him. At the same time I realized the front of the aircraft seemed to drop; the plane was going into a dive. I had to seal the breach in the hull with a shield. Unfortunately the plane pitched to the right as I tried to focus on the breach. I was thrown sideways.

Both Dan and I landed in the laps of a married couple who were desperately scrambling to work out how to position the oxygen masks. One of them was trying to place it on their young daughter; the girl's face was filled with absolute terror.

The instructions always tell you to put the mask on yourself first, I thought. *Then help younger children. Don't people read the instruction cards?*

People didn't always think well in a panic. Fortunately I had my ability to manipulate air, so I created an air bubble around myself and Dan. We could breathe. For now. I grabbed one of the masks and positioned it over the man's face while Dan helped him to aid the girl.

He gave us a grateful look as the air began to flow. Regaining my feet, I realized the plane was now rising again. For a few seconds it seemed level. Then the nose continued to rise.

'The pilots must be trying to get control of the plane,' I said to Dan.

'You've got to seal the hole,' Dan yelled.

I tried to focus on creating a shield in the hull. Usually when I created shields I could see them as a faint out of focus bubble. I held out my hand and focused hard on knitting the air molecules together that would create the barrier. Nothing was happening.

'Come on,' I groaned in desperation. 'Work!'

Still, the shield would not form.

What was wrong with my powers?

Before I could dwell on the issue further, I saw a crack appearing in the hull next to the breach. It looked like the whole plane was starting to tear apart.

I had to seal that hole in the hull, but nothing was happening.

'Take a breath!' I told Dan.

He looked at me in confusion, but followed my command. I dropped the air bubbles around us and put all my focus into creating the shield. The hull continued to tear, ripping into a window next to an elderly woman.

The shield would not form.

I cast a despairing look across the rows of seats. I could see Chad staring at me in confusion. The preferred option was for me to create one of my shields. It was invisible and while people might wonder later how the plane held together it would forever remain a mystery.

The second option was Chad.

With my powers out of commission, it was time for option two.

I nodded to Chad and he immediately pointed at the break in the hull. Ice started to form at its edges. Within seconds it had crept across the gap and covered the hull. The terrible screaming wind that had filled the cabin dropped away to silence. Even the terrible cold subsided. The temperature outside the hull had probably been below zero. Now it was slowly starting to rise.

A groan sounded throughout the entire plane. Chad had sealed the breach, but it sounded like irreversible damage had been done to the fuselage of the aircraft. The whole plane would rip apart in seconds.

I caught the eye of the stewardess we had just spoken to—Kelly—and she opened her eyes in horror. Someone came racing down the aisle, pushing Kelly out of the way and almost knocking me over.

Ebony.

I instantly realized what she intended to do. I

chased her down the aisle. She positioned herself next to the icy barrier that her brother had created.

'What are you making?' I asked.

'Titanium.'

She placed her hand against the ice and the barrier immediately began to change color. It was changing to a shade of dull silver. Within moments Ebony had used her transmutation ability to strengthen the plug.

'It's one of the strongest and lightest metals known to man,' Ebony said. 'I'm changing most of the hull as well.'

The terrible groaning that had affected the hull subsided. I was just about ready to relax slightly when I realized the plane was veering wildly to one side again.

Chad and Brodie joined us.

'What's going on with the plane?' Chad asked. 'Why can't the pilots get it under control?'

'I'm not sure,' I said.

Kelly, the stewardess, joined our group. Her eyes opened as wide as plates.

'What's going on back here?' Her mouth fell open. 'How did you fix the hull?'

'We didn't do anything,' I said. 'It just fixed itself.'

Okay, it was the worst explanation in history, but I didn't have another option at the time.

The plane veered back level again, but began to go back into a dive.

'Why isn't the plane leveling out?' I asked.

'I don't know,' she said. 'Maybe some other damage occurred when the explosion happened.'

'It's the tail,' a voice came from down the aisle.

We grouped around a couple of seats where a man was peering out the window toward the rear of the plane.

'I think debris hit the tail,' he said. 'It looks like part of it is missing.'

Brodie pushed past him and looked out the window.

'We need—' She began.

Before she could say anything more, the

plane's nose abruptly began to rise again. Someone nearby dragged off their air mask and vomited.

'I know,' Chad said. 'We need a new tail.'

He looked through the window and focused. A few seconds later he moved out of the way and Ebony took his place at the window.

She smiled. 'One new tail. Not as good as the first, but good enough so we can land.'

Kelly looked at us in amazement. 'Who are you kids? How did you do that?'

Some of the other passengers were looking at us in amazement. I looked to Dan. He nodded to me without speaking.

'I'll explain,' he said. 'Just as soon as we land.'

The major airport servicing Las Vegas is McCarran International Airport. Half an hour after the plane had landed, Dan positioned himself at the front door as people exited the plane. Upon landing, Ebony had already turned the appropriate parts of the 747 back to their original substances. She evaporated the tail and the hole in the side of the plane.

'You will forget any of us were ever on board this plane,' Dan told the departing passengers.

People smiled and nodded in return.

'You were never here,' an elderly man told him.

'We've never seen you before in our lives,' an entire family chimed in unison as they marched past us.

'The force will be with you,' Dan said cheekily. 'Always.'

As the last of the passengers disembarked, Kelly and a few of the other stewardesses grouped around us.

'The pilots have to be congratulated for landing the plane under such terrible conditions,' Dan said.

'We will congratulate them,' they said in unison.

'You will forget us completely and emphasize the bravery and ability of the pilots,' he said.

The crew agreed.

'You might remember one very handsome

young man who showed exceptional bravery under extremely—'

That's when we grabbed Dan and disembarked. He's a talented kid, but sometimes he doesn't know when to stop.

Chapter Four

Home sweet home.

It was late in the afternoon. The drive back across the desert in the campervan was mostly in silence. Brodie drove. No-one even bothered to turn on the radio. Facing death has that sort of effect on you.

My eyes were firmly on the changing landscape. Las Vegas sits in the Mojave Desert. It's a barren place. Hot and dry. But it has its own beauty. When we first came here there was an almost unanimous vote to live in a hotel in the middle of town. It was only through my constant arguing and stubbornness that we ended up living to the west on Highway One Sixty.

As we turned off the highway onto a side road, my mind returned to the events on the plane.

What had happened to my powers? I had never had problems with them before. While at The Agency I had been able to form shields and weapons with ease. Was it something on the plane? Was it the stress of the situation?

Our campervan crested a rise and we saw our little home in the valley. It wasn't much, but it suited us.

Or maybe I should rephrase that. It wasn't much, but it suited me. We pulled up outside the house. It was a single story bungalow with views over the long, rolling hills. Low lying scrub surrounded the place on all sides. It had a number of water tanks as well as an outdoor spa and solar power.

Brodie brought the campervan to a halt. The others piled out through the side doors. Brodie and I sat silently in the front. We watched Chad leading the others inside. A minute later music erupted from the interior.

Nice to see someone was having a good time.

'What happened back on the plane?' Brodie asked.

'What do you mean?'

'You know what I mean.'

So she had noticed. 'I don't know. I tried focusing on forming a shield in the door, but I couldn't make it happen.'

'Don't give yourself a hard time,' she said gently. 'It was hard for everyone to focus.'

'Everyone still did their job,' I replied. 'Everyone except me.'

She reached over and touched my hand with the tips of her fingers. It was like a spark of electricity. Brodie and I were not officially an item, but she still had the power to make me turn to jello. I turned my hand over so her fingers lay in my palm. Taking her hand in mine, I leant across the seat and gently kissed her lips.

Pushing her lips against mine, I felt dizzy as I closed my eyes and surrendered myself to the moment.

I wish it could have lasted forever, but at that moment I heard a distant sound. Brodie drew away from me. We climbed from the vehicle and rounded the campervan. Walking up the road to the crest of the hill, we saw a car making its way toward us. A black four wheel drive.

We stood at the top of the hill, watching it as

it grew nearer. Visitors out here were unknown. It was possible someone had taken the wrong turn off the highway.

Possible, but unlikely.

By now I could see the windows of the vehicle were made of darkened glass. It was impossible to see the occupants.

The vehicle drew to a halt.

Footsteps in the dirt sounded from behind me. Chad, Ebony, Dan and Ferdy had come out to see who had taken the long drive from Vegas just to see us.

Both the front doors of the vehicle opened. For a moment nothing happened. Then two men stepped out.

I recognized both of them immediately.

Mr. Jones and Mr. Brown.

From The Agency.

Chapter Five

These Americans love their flashing lights, General Wolff thought as he stepped from the interior of the Cadillac.

He was standing at the corner of Tropicana Avenue and Las Vegas Boulevard in the heart of Las Vegas. Night had fallen. He cast a critical eye around him. Some of the most famous hotels in the city lay around him; the Luxor, the MGM Grand, the Excalibur, the Monte Carlo. Symbols of opulence and wealth.

And flashing lights.

Lots of flashing lights.

For Wolff who had grown up in poverty and had once killed another child for half a loaf of moldy bread, the sight was yet another reminder of how far he had come. He allowed himself a few seconds to take in the sights. Then he reminded himself that possessions were nothing unless they could be defended and he shut the images from his mind.

He had a man to meet.

His personal finances had taken a blow since The Agency had attacked his operation on Cayo Placetas. The organization that he had once commanded—Typhoid—had fallen apart at the seams. One of his former commanders had taken charge of it. Wolff doubted Typhoid would ever reach its former glory.

For Wolff, his concerns were of a far more financial nature. His payment for the project on Cayo Placetas had never eventuated and now he was operating from long held savings in a bank account on the Cayman Islands.

He was far from poor, but neither was he as wealthy as he would have liked.

Mercer Todd's one hundred million dollars would help to put him back on top, but he could not do it alone. To even start recruiting the team required for the operation, Wolff would need a man with special abilities.

So many times in life, Wolff had found, success depended on knowing just the right people.

If you didn't know the right people, you had

to find those who did.

He chose to walk the short distance to his hotel. He was staying at The Luxor, the second largest hotel in Las Vegas. Shaped like a pyramid, it was named after the ancient city of Luxor in Egypt. Within, the structure was hollow, lined with hundreds of apartments. He ignored the doorman, walking through the main entrance and walked straight to the reception desk.

Many men would be impressed by this, he thought. *But I am not like many men.*

He booked in and stashed his single bag into his room before going to the Liquidity Bar located at the center of the Casino floor. The man he was looking for was sitting alone nursing a drink and eyeing a group of laughing women at the bar. He noticed Wolff from across the room.

'General Wolff,' he said. 'It's been too long.'

'Mr. Tate.' He shook the man's hand. 'And my name is Rudolf Wills.'

'Rudolf Wills,' Tate mused. 'It has a ring to it. Certainly better than that name you were using in

Afghanistan that time. What was it..?'

'Hyde.' Even Wolff had to laugh at the thought. 'It seemed a good idea at the time.'

Both men sipped at their drinks in silence for a moment. There was something that Wolff had forgotten about Tate. He was cold. Not his personality. His skin. Unnaturally cold. His skin had a healthy enough pallor. His eyes were the picture of good health. Yet he always felt clammy to the touch. Like stroking the interior of a refrigerator.

Tate sat his drink down. 'So you have an operation in the works.'

Wolff nodded.

'And you need some personnel?'

'Yes.'

'How many?'

'Five or six,' Wolff said. 'I'm going up against some modified humans. Six teenagers. But powerful.'

Tate lapsed into thought for a moment. 'Five or six should be enough.'

'Are we talking the same kind of associates?'

Wolff asked.

Tate said a particular word that would have made most people react in horror or burst into disbelieving laughter.

Wolff did neither. 'Yes,' he said. 'We're talking about the same people.'

Tate glanced at his watch. 'We need to meet a man at a bar across town. He will arrange the personnel, but we must take along an offer of good faith.'

Wolff nodded. 'An offer?'

'A gift,' Tate confirmed. 'I'll arrange it.'

The two men left the bar. Tate requested his vehicle through valet parking and a few minutes later an enclosed van was delivered to the front entrance. Tate drove them through the city to one of the more squalid parts of Las Vegas. This part of the city was rarely seen by the tourists. Wolff noted it had none of the flashing lights of the main strip. In fact, lights were rather a rarity in this area.

Tate stopped the van at the side of a road. It was a quiet backstreet. He produced a tranquilizer gun from the glove compartment. Wolff had never seen one so small; mostly they were rifles. Then the two men waited. After a few minutes Wolff noticed a girl walking quickly through the area. Tate waited till she almost drew level with the van. Then he opened his window and fired once at the back of the girl.

She gave a small cry, staggered a couple of feet and collapsed.

Tate climbed from his seat, went over to her, threw her over his shoulder and tossed her in the back of the van. He gagged her then padlocked her hands and feet. Climbing back behind the wheel of the van, he restarted the engine and continued down the quiet street.

The whole abduction had taken less than sixty seconds.

Wolff turned around and looked through a small window showing the back. He could not see the girl. He peered from side to side.

'Where—'

'There is a false floor in the back,' Tate said. 'Even if we are stopped by the police they will discover nothing.'

The man thinks of everything, Wolff thought. *Good.*

They drove another ten minutes until they reached a bar in another darkened street. Out of half a dozen street lights, only two were left working and even these seemed almost dulled by the constant pressure of the darkness. At first Wolff could not see any life at all on the street. It looked like every single business had permanently closed its doors. Then he realized a faint illuminated sign hung over a door.

Joe's Bar

A man stood in front of the building. It was impossible to determine if he was a customer or a bouncer. Tate stopped the vehicle outside the bar. He and Wolff climbed out. Tate went to the rear of the van and a moment later emerged with the unconscious girl over his shoulder. The man outside the bar opened the door and allowed them inside.

Much to Wolff's surprise, the interior was the image of opulence. The bar itself appeared to be made from mahogany. The chairs were black leather.

Floating candles in clear glass bowls sat in the center of the tables. Pictures of many of the early movers and shakers of Las Vegas—Frank Sinatra, Dean Martin among them—adorned the walls of the establishment. Music played gently in the background.

Wolff recognized it as Sammy Davis Jnr.

A number of men and women were sitting and drinking. No-one looked up when they entered. As Tate carried the unconscious woman through the premises, everyone treated it as if it were the most normal thing on the planet.

Possibly, here, it was.

A man sat alone in a booth at the far end. He looked up when they approached and inclined his head in greeting. Like every other occupant of the bar, he ignored the woman completely.

'Good evening, Mr. Tate,' the stranger said. 'It's been too long.'

'It has indeed,' Tate said. 'May I introduce my friend, Rudolf Wills? Rudolf, this is Jacob.'

Jacob. No last name. Possibly he didn't need

one.

'I'm sure there's no need for falsities around Jacob,' Wolff said. 'I am known as General Solomon Wolff. You may have heard of me.'

'I have.'

'General Wolff has an operation in the works,' Tate said. 'He is looking for five or six of your people to participate.'

'What sort of operation is it?' Jacob asked.

Wolff described it.

Jacob thought about it for a moment. Then he said, 'The price is ten million paid to me. I will distribute the funds accordingly to my associates.'

'Naturally,' Wolff said.

He was pleased. This was going better than he expected. At that moment the unconscious girl gave a shudder. She raised her head. Peered about uncertainly. Her eyes filled with alarm. Just as she opened her mouth to scream, Jacob reached across and placed a finger across her lips as if to silence her.

'Look at the flame,' Jacob said.

She looked at the flame in the center of the

table.

Amazing, Wolff thought.

The girl said nothing. She did not flinch. She did not move a muscle. She simply stared at the flame. She kept her eyes focused on it. She did not look away for a second of the fifteen minutes it took Jacob to kill her.

Sammy Davis Junior continued to croon softly in the background the whole time.

Chapter Six

Oddly, I was not displeased to see either Mr. Jones or Mr. Brown. Certainly none of us trusted Mr. Jones as far as we could throw him—and in Ferdy's case that was a considerable distance—but Mr. Brown had been my personal trainer. He had taught me many of the skills I now took for granted. I would not have survived my time on Cayo Placetas if it were not for him.

Maybe he or Mr. Jones would have an insight into why my abilities seemed erratic.

'You weren't kidding when you said you wanted to get away from it all,' Mr. Jones said as he followed us into the house. 'This is about as far away from civilization you can get without living in a cave.'

'I would have preferred somewhere in the city,' Chad said. 'But our venerated leader wanted us to stay out of sight.'

'Out of sight is good,' Mr. Jones said. 'Staying out of sight has kept mods alive for centuries.'

'Mods?' Brodie asked.

'Mods are humans that have been modified in one way or another,' Jones said.

'We're not the first?' I asked.

'Not at all,' Jones replied.

'You didn't tell us that before,' Brodie said.

'You didn't give me a chance,' Mr. Jones said. 'It's a shame you left The Agency when you did. We had barely started your training. There are still so many things for you to learn.'

'I saw how you taught Ferdy,' I said, my voice growing hard. 'That left a sour taste in my mouth.'

When I had found Ferdy he had been languishing in a tiny cell alone under the earth. He had barely been treated like a human being.

'Sour is one of the basic tastes in the ancient healing science known as Ayurveda,' Ferdy spoke up. 'The others are sweet, bitter, salty, pungent and astringent.' He looked at both the men. 'You are Mr. Jones, but Ferdy doesn't know you.'

'I'm Mr. Brown,' the military man said. 'How

are you, Ferdy?'

'Ferdy is fine,' he replied. 'The word Mr. originates from medieval times.'

Brown nodded.

I wasn't sure how Mr. Brown felt about being here. I had the sense he seemed a little uncomfortable. Last time we were on his turf; The Agency's training ground. Now the shoe was on the other foot.

'What brings you here?' Ebony asked.

I was a little surprised to hear Ebony speak. She was usually so quiet you forgot she was even in the room. She had changed a little over the last few months, however, as she had taken Ferdy under her wing. Maybe the responsibility had made her more confident.

'You expressed some interest in helping The Agency should the need arise,' Mr. Jones said. 'The need has arisen.'

Chad laughed. 'The need has arisen? Really? That sounds so dramatic. You can use that when they make the television series.' He shook his head. 'There's not enough need in the world to take me back there. You people tried to kill us last time.'

'That's not true,' Mr. Jones said. 'Twelve was responsible for the abuses in the Alpha Project.'

'What's that old saying?' Brodie asked 'Dead men—or dead aliens—tell no tales? It's easy to blame things on dead people.'

It was interesting to see everyone's reaction to Mr. Jones's suggestion. I understood how they felt. The Agency had been responsible for taking each of us from our homelands and filling us full of experimental drugs to see what would happen.

Of course, the same drugs had turned other teenagers into dead teenagers and had turned Ferdy into—

Well, we weren't really too sure. He was Ferdy. Brilliant but unable to carry on a conversation. Strong enough to lift a tank, but sometimes unable to work out how to open a door.

'Twelve took the original aims of The Alpha Project and twisted them,' Mr. Jones said. 'He was a rogue among the Bakari. That project is finished. Now we want to move forward—'

'So you're not torturing and killing any more teenagers,' Ebony interrupted. Red splotches of fury decorated her cheeks. 'No more destroying of lives. No more stealing kids from their parents.'

Mr. Jones stopped and bit his bottom lip.

It was Mr. Brown who spoke next. 'We're here because we need your help.'

'What sort of help?' I asked.

'A canister of a deadly virus has been stolen,' Mr. Brown said. 'At the moment, the canister is locked by a sophisticated encryption code.'

'Very sophisticated,' Mr. Jones piped up. 'It is virtually impossible to open.'

'So?' Chad sounded bored. He was actually inspecting his nails. 'Why are you so concerned if it can't be opened?'

'I said it's virtually impossible,' Mr. Jones said. 'There is still a very slight chance it can be opened and used.'

'And what would happen then?' I asked.

'You may have heard of the H5N1 virus,' Mr. Jones said.

'Uh, is that the bird flu?' Brodie asked.

'It's commonly known as Avian Influenza or Bird Flu,' Mr. Brown confirmed. 'It has a mortality rate of sixty percent.'

'Sixty percent?' Chad said. 'That doesn't sound so bad.'

It did to me. 'That's sixty people in a hundred,' I said. 'It's six hundred million people out of a billion. Out of the current world's population it would be three point six billion people.'

'Wow,' Chad said. 'You can add. Can you multiply as well?'

I ignored him. 'Is that what this is? H5N1?'

Mr. Jones shook his head. 'The weakness of H5N1 is that it is not airborne.'

'Good for us,' Brodie said. 'Bad for the virus.'

'Absolutely,' Mr. Jones said. 'It is its current saving grace. Unfortunately scientists in Germany recently tweaked the virus to see how difficult it would be to make it airborne.'

'What a clever thing to do,' I said

sarcastically. 'Take a lethal virus and make it more efficient.'

Mr. Brown seemed to be of a similar opinion. 'The scientists claimed their reason to do so was to plan ahead in case the virus should ever mutate of its own accord.'

'They were successful in their attempts,' Mr. Jones said. 'Wildly successful. The resulting virus is known as Doomsday.'

I was sort of wondering about the definition of wildly successful. It sounded a little like a doctor successfully removing a bullet from a patient—but the patient dying on the operating table.

'Not only were they able to make it airborne, but they were able to make it far more lethal.' Mr. Jones paused. 'One hundred percent lethal.'

One hundred percent lethal. That sounded like the same stupid mode of thinking that had driven The Alpha Project. Let's take some perfectly harmless teenagers, inject them with a weird combination of drugs and see what happens.

'So if this virus gets free...' Brodie said

slowly.

'It will kill every human being on Earth,' Mr. Brown said. 'Every man, woman and child.'

Chad shook his head slowly. 'It sounds like you guys have got a real problem. I'm off to see what's on the tube. I think there're reruns of CSI.'

'Chad—' I started.

He spread his arms. 'We're the victims, leader man. You need to get that through your stupid skull. All of you. We had lives before these clowns used us as mice.'

'Mice are a type of mammal,' Ferdy said.

'I'm with Chad on this one,' Ebony said. 'I have no desire to go back to The Agency or ever have anything to do with you people.' She took Ferdy's hand. 'Want to play on the computer again?'

'Ferdy likes chess,' he said.

They stood and left the room.

I looked at Brodie. 'What do you think?'

'I'm sorry.' She looked directly at Mr. Jones and Mr. Brown. 'I just don't trust you guys.'

'Dan?' I asked.

He shook his head. 'Not without you guys.'

'What about you, Axel?' Mr. Jones asked. 'You must realize the seriousness of this situation. Not just for you, but for every person on Earth.'

My eyes strayed to the dark desert outside. The wind had started to weave its way across the dry landscape. This was a place of contrasts. Stifling heat during the day. Freezing cold at night.

'We work as a team,' I said. 'Or not at all.'

Chapter Seven

It seems, General Wolff thought, *that I spend most of my life at airports.*

This time he was at Henderson Executive Airport. It was smaller than McCarran International. Many single engine planes were housed here. Many private jets. There were times when it was better to remain under the radar; this was one of those times.

The meeting with Jacob had gone well; his team was on their way from Mexico and would arrive at any moment. If the arrangement with Jacob had not transpired, there were other people Wolff could have contacted; all mods of various abilities. Some were better than others. Jacob and his people just happened to have an excellent reputation for being both efficient and ruthless. Like all mods everywhere, they had remained secret over the years.

Now it appeared all that was about to change.

There had been rumblings among the members of the United Nations Security Council that the time had come for mods to 'come out of the closet'. Wolff had his doubts about the wisdom of this course of action. Anonymity was a strength. Why give away such an advantage when it was unnecessary?

However, technology had increased so much—especially in the last twenty years—that keeping mods a secret was becoming more difficult by the day. Everyone had a cell phone. Every second person had a blog. Combine the two and it meant that everyone was a pseudo journalist. People were using Twitter and Facebook to start revolutions.

Maybe I'm getting old, Wolff thought. *Maybe I'll retire after this operation. Maybe.*

Planes were arriving at the airport all the time; a long procession of small aircraft that were landing and being bedded down for the night or lifting off to continue to destinations unknown. Wolff watched as a particular plane appeared, first as a bright dot in the sky. It grew ever larger. Zooming in to land, it finally taxied into the hanger where he waited.

The aircraft looked to be little more than a twelve seater. It seemed likely Jacob's crew used it to traverse the country to carry out their operations. A good method of operation. Fly in for the kill—so to speak—and then fly straight back out again while the hapless local law enforcement agencies searched the local environ looking for the perpetrators.

A few minutes passed and then the side door dropped down and the occupants disembarked. Wolff drew in a breath. There were five of them. Three men. Two women. They all looked to be aged in their twenties. They looked like an ordinary group of executives, dressed in expensive suits and business attire. The men looked like they could be lawyers. The women could have been their personal assistants.

Wolff had to hand it to them; they were professionals. There was nothing about the group to suggest they were anything other than a typical group of business people traveling across the country to attend a meeting in Las Vegas.

'I'm Anthony,' the tallest of the group introduced himself. He had a soft voice and a firm handshake. 'These are my associates. Michael. John. Ramona. Elizabeth.'

The General introduced himself.

'Wolff,' Anthony mused. 'I knew a Ferdinand Wolff at the Battle of Chickamauga. Any relation?'

'Possibly.' Wolff reached into his pocket. 'I have the address here for the operation.'

Anthony took the piece of paper from him and read it. 'We'll do this tonight.'

'Tonight?'

'Is that too soon?'

'Not at all,' Wolff said. 'The sooner the better.'

'What are the abilities of these mods?' Anthony asked.

Wolff described them.

'Good,' Anthony said. 'It doesn't sound like anything we can't handle.'

Chapter Eight

I opened my eyes to darkness.

For a few confusing seconds I thought I was still asleep. I had been dreaming about wheat fields. The same dream had been returning night after night for months. I was in a wheat field walking to a farmhouse in the distance. A boy was sitting on the front steps. As I drew closer he stood and started toward me. His face blurred. The dream ended and I awoke. I found myself staring up at the ceiling in the darkness.

My eyes shifted to the digital clock next to my bed.

3.14am

Great. I lay in the bed and listened to the silence. I knew the sounds of the desert. The wind sweeping over the hills. A piece of metal that rattled on the porch. Tonight there seemed to be none of that.

Still, I could hear something. A crackling sound.

Climbing out of bed, I threw some clothes on

and wandered down the passageway. A light was on in Brodie's room down the hall. Her door was open. Brodie appeared in the doorway.

'Do you hear that?' she asked quietly.

'What is it?'

'Sounds like a fire.'

'Out here?'

Another light snapped on down the hall. Chad blearily appeared with his hair askew. He never looked his best first thing in the morning. He looked even worse now.

'Whassgoingon?' he asked. 'Whassthenoise?'

'We're not sure,' Brodie said. 'Sounds like a fire.'

Chad mumbled something and disappeared back into his room. I wasn't sure what that meant, so we continued onto the porch. The night was dark, but the glow of Las Vegas still illuminated the night sky. Other nearby towns also bleached their glow into the sky.

'What's that over there?' Brodie asked.

Another glow lay between nearby hills. I had

never seen it before. We started across the desert. After a few moments, Brodie grabbed my arm.

'Wouldn't it be faster if we flew?' she asked.

'I'm not sure if I trust—'

'Let's worry about that later. Someone might be in trouble.'

I formed an invisible force field. We climbed aboard and zoomed across the desert. Brodie was right. By the time we flew over the crest of the hill we could see what had caused the fire. A car lay overturned by the side of the road.

'Hell,' I said.

'Bring us in close.'

We came in to land directly next to the vehicle. Cars rarely came this way. It was one of those roads that literally led nowhere. Brodie and I had followed it one day. It simply trailed off after a couple of miles into the desert. I'm not sure it even had a name.

The car was alight and had been in flames for some time. Maybe this was what had awoken us; the sound of the car flipping on the road. There was no-one in the vehicle. Maybe they had been thrown free.

We started searching all around the area looking for the driver. We should have brought flashlights. At that moment the sound of footsteps crunching across the dry earth caught our attention.

'Thanks for waiting!' Chad yelled. He had brought two flashlights with him so we started to systematically search the area by dividing it into a grid pattern. The minutes passed slowly. The car continued to burn. We extended the search area and searched that too.

This made no sense.

'Where is the driver?' Brodie asked.

'Maybe he was able to walk away and he's walking back to Vegas,' Chad said. 'Sometimes people walk away from some pretty bad accidents.'

'Maybe.' I was still unconvinced. We went back to the car and searched for footprints around the wreck. If they existed it was too dark to see them. The driver's side door had broken off in the crash. I turned it over in the darkness.

'Bring the flashlight over here,' I asked Chad.

He shone it on the door. All three of us peered at a mark in the center of the door. There was no denying what it looked like, but that was impossible.

'It looks like a footprint,' Brodie said.

'So the driver crashed his car,' Chad said. 'And then kicked the door off its hinges.'

'That would take superhuman strength,' I said. 'How is that possible?'

'Something else makes no sense either,' Chad said. 'What's this car doing out here? No-one comes out here in the middle of the day let alone at night.'

'Maybe someone wanted to draw us out here,' Brodie suggested.

A chill ran up and down my spine. 'Not to draw us here.'

'What—' Chad started.

I looked back to the house. 'To draw us away.'

Chapter Nine

Ebony had awoken in the darkness with no idea as to what roused her from her sleep. At first she thought it was someone using the bathroom, but there was no sound of the toilet flushing. All the lights were out. The entire house lay in silence. She glanced at the clock.

3:30am

What the hell?

This was way too early to be awake. Lying on her side, she closed her eyes again. Time to go back to sleep.

Except a noise was coming from the door.

She always slept with her door open. She liked air to circulate through her room at night. She kept her window open too, but it was permanently locked so that only two or three inches were open at the bottom.

The sound coming from her door sounded like scratching. Could it be a rat? There were various types of small animals that lived in the desert. Maybe something had come in from outside. Tilting her head ever so slightly, she peered over to the door and saw only blackness.

Something hit the side of her dressing table.

What the—?

Moving her line of sight away from the doorway, she tried to see her dressing table, but found it impossible without moving her head. Now the sound seemed to find purchase on the wall. It slowly ascended until there was a slight bump as it reached the ceiling. She dared not move a muscle. She had no idea what it was, but it was large. She knew that by the way it collided with the ceiling.

Could it be a bird? But no bird could be so large. What the hell was it?

Only now did she allow herself to move her head slightly in the darkness. She did so with infinitesimal movement. One tiny fraction of an inch at a time. Whatever it was in the room could not possibly detect the slow movement.

Could it?

Her eyes moved to the ceiling above her

dressing table. All she saw was darkness. One large patch of darkness. The longer she stared at the darkness, the more she thought it odd.

Why was that one patch so dark? It seemed to be blacker than—

Something moved past her door.

It took every bit of control for Ebony to bite back a scream. Whoever—or whatever—it was that had moved by had done so in complete silence. It had done so without even making the sound of a foot tread on the timber floors. Like a ghost.

How was such a thing possible?

Now Ebony returned her gaze to the space above her dressing table and she felt a growing horror that chilled her to the soul.

The patch above the dressing table was no longer in darkness. If anything, the ceiling looked uniformly dark. She shifted her eyes again to the dressing table next to her bed. Her bedside lamp was within reach. Within her bedside drawer lay a gun. Dan had been able to procure it for her from a gun dealer in town. The poor man had thought he was selling it to a husband and wife from Tallahassee instead of a pair of teenagers with no identification.

Another sound came from the ceiling.

Directly above her.

Ebony had never felt such terror in her life.

The dark shape that had hovered over her dressing table now hovered directly over her bed. It clung to the ceiling directly over her. To make matters worse she thought she could make out some detail. In its own strange way it looked like a spider.

An enormous spider.

She felt sick.

I have super powers, Ebony reminded herself. I can transmute a substance into anything of my choosing. I can turn a human being into salt if necessary. I can turn lead into gold.

She had even spoken to Chad about how she could use non lethal force against people if necessary. A person would be rendered immobile if she grabbed their clothing—their shirt, for instance—and transformed it into steel. They would be stuck in position, unable to make a move.

Think steel, she told herself. Think steel.

Just as she decided to reach across and turn her lamp on, the shape on the ceiling shifted position slightly. Two tiny red balls of light came to life directly above her. Ebony felt her heart chugging like a steam engine. Her whole body grew rigid as if she were slowly turning to ice.

Eyes.

A pair of glowing red eyes peered down from the ceiling at her.

Her left arm shot out and grabbed the light switch for the lamp. She snapped it on. At the same time she reached up with her hand.

'Steel!' she snapped. 'St—'

She got no further. A man lay back comfortably on the ceiling staring down at her. He was naked except for a pair of leather briefs. He appeared to be about twenty-five years of age, clean shaven, muscular and very pale. In the darkness his eyes had burned bright red, but now the light was on they were black. Even the normally white pupils were black. It was like looking at someone who had two perfectly black balls in their eye sockets instead of their eyes.

He smiled.

There was nothing nice about that smile.

Ebony decided to scream. She was good at screaming. The sound would wake the entire household. She got as far as drawing back her breath. Then she looked into the man's eyes and saw he loved her.

He really, really loved her. It was a timeless love. An eternal love. For as long as she lived she would never find a love like this. Their love would exist from now till all life faded on Earth. Even now time seemed to fall away. The man leapt down from the ceiling and landed nimbly on his feet next to her bed. His eyes remained on her the whole time.

'My name is Anthony,' he said. 'And you are?'

'Ebony.'

'Ebony. Such a beautiful name.' He held out his hand. 'Arise.'

Ebony pushed back her sheet, placed her feet

on the floor and stood before him.

'Do you know how long I searched for you?' he asked.

'Forever,' Ebony said. She knew that. Anthony had searched far and wide for his one true love and now he had found her and she had found him and they would be joined for all time. It was a love that no man could tear asunder. It had been said that love was a drug. If it was, she was an addict.

His eyes continued to bore into her and now she knew she had to offer herself to him completely. She had to be owned by him for their love to be consummated and there was only one way for that to happen.

She tilted her head, offering her neck to him. Anthony smiled and she smelt his breath. One part of her mind told her his breath was rotten. Fetid. Like road kill on the side of a busy highway in the middle of summer.

She didn't care.

Love was like that.

'Time to—'

Before Anthony had a chance to complete the sentence, a fist appeared from nowhere and collided with the side of his head. The impact was so massive his entire body slammed into her bedside table and continued into the wall until he was jammed into the gap. He let out a shriek of rage as he struggled to escape the wall.

Ferdy pulled him out of the gap and with no effort at all, threw him through the window. He fell into the night beyond.

Ebony regained her senses just in time to understand Ferdy's words.

'Vampires,' he said. 'Originating from the early Serbian word vampir meaning a dead creature known to drink blood.'

Chapter Ten

By the time we reached the house we were just in time to see a figure being thrown through the window. A man. He rolled twice, leapt to his feet and yelled in a foreign language. He sprang up from the ground and jumped.

Straight up onto the roof.

'What the hell—' I started.

'He yelled something in German,' Chad said. 'Something about us returning. There must be others in the house.'

The man raced along the top of the roof as nimbly as a cat. I started after him, landing a few feet behind him. He turned around and aimed a fist at my head.

Smack!

I didn't even see it coming. One second I was reaching for him. The next the blow almost took off the top of my head. I hit the roof, rolled off and only just threw up a shield in time to stop myself from slamming into the ground. As soon as I righted myself I felt the impact of something landing on my back. An arm encircled my neck.

The man was trying to bite me!

I focused on creating a blast of air and hit him firmly in the face with it. He flew backwards into the darkness.

By now lights were coming on all over the house. I saw Ebony through her window struggling with another of the figures. It was a girl clad in a leather bra and shorts. Ferdy was holding another of the creatures around the neck.

The man came racing toward me from the darkness. He had his mouth open. I could see large incisors—

Fire leapt out of the darkness and engulfed him.

He shrieked in agony and I felt someone pushing me down.

'They're vampires,' Chad said.

'How do you know?' I asked, watching the figure rolling around on the ground.

'What else would they be?'

I remembered the teeth.

Okay. They were vampires.

He gave the burning vampire another blast and then turned to climb through Ebony's window. I followed him. Ebony was trying unsuccessfully to turn her vampire to salt. Where her hands touched the creature, I could see large patches of salt, but the substance was not spreading to the rest of the creature.

The vampire turned its head and I saw her eyes.

I suddenly wondered why we were fighting them. Especially this girl. I felt I had been searching for her my entire life and now—

Chad engulfed her head in a block of ice.

The spell faded.

'They're vampires,' Ebony shouted, breaking me free of the creature. 'They can mesmerize you!'

They can mesmerize you.

I remembered the ancient legends. Which meant they could brainwash you in a fashion similar to Dan. That was one of their legendary powers. And supposedly they had the strength of ten men. And they could turn into bats.

But how much of it was legend and how much was true? The vampire in Ferdy's grasp seemed helpless. Whatever autism Ferdy suffered from made him invincible to their mesmerizing powers. Ferdy had his hand firmly around the creature's neck.

Movement in the hallway caught my attention. I saw Brodie falling back past the door with one of the creatures on her back as another one attacked her from in front. I climbed over the bed, focused on creating a blast of air and slammed it into the creature's head. It went sideways through the wall.

I didn't know how many of these creatures were in the house, but there was a chance we were getting the upper hand.

Then the lights went out.

Chad set fire to the ceiling. I understood his intention. We could not fight if we could not see what we were up against. I pursued the creature into the next room as I heard a fire alarm sound. It was not a back-to-base alarm. The fire brigade would not attend unless someone dialed 911.

The creature that I had smashed through the wall had ended up in the living room. Now it scampered up onto the wall and into the recesses of the ceiling. It was so dark in here the visibility was reduced to a few feet. I could hear fighting going in the hallway. It sounded like Brodie was involved in a full pitched battle. I heard another blast of flame from Chad. An inhuman shriek erupted from the room behind me. Maybe that was another creature on fire.

A sound came from the ceiling above and behind me. I formed a blast of air—a focused ball of wind—and fired it at the ceiling. It punched a hole straight through the roof and into the night, but missed the vampire.

Something slammed into me from behind. It was like being hit by a truck. My face hit the living room table and I tasted blood in my mouth. The hissing creature grabbed me and threw me across the room. I hit the wall and slid to the floor.

I tried to form a shield, but I could not focus. What was going on with my powers? I could not make it happen. Within seconds the creature had leapt across the room like a giant frog and landed in front of me. It picked me up effortlessly as I tried to create another ball of air.

Its breath was terrible. Like rotten meat. I punched it hard in the face and it laughed. I struggled to create a shield between me and it, but nothing would happen.

'Come on!' a voice yelled from the hallway. 'We only need the boy!'

The vampire gave me a last look and threw me across the room. I hit my head. Stunned, I lay there for several moments. I could hear the fire spreading. Something collapsed in the building. I heard the distant roar of a vehicle.

I have to get out of here, I thought. *I have to move.*

I rose unsteadily to my feet. Where were the others? Someone appeared in my field of vision. It was Chad.

'Quick!' he said. 'They're getting away!'

He dragged me out of the building and into the

night. The cold air snapped me back to wakefulness. I looked back at the house. It was completely alight now. All of our possessions—what there were of them—were inside the burning structure.

Chad held up something in his hand. 'I was able to grab the book.'

The book. The one containing all the addresses.

But where were our friends?

'What about Brodie?' I gripped Chad's arm. 'And Dan and—'

'They're gone!' he said. 'They were thrown into a truck and taken away.' He looked into the night. 'We're the only ones left.'

Chapter Eleven

'They've got a head start on us,' Chad said. 'But it's only a couple of minutes. You need to create a flying platform so we can catch up.'

That was easier said than done.

In my mind I created the flying wedge I had formed a hundred times before. I saw it perfectly; an arrowhead of shimmering air that would support us as we soared up into the sky. I had made it so many times it even had its wings angled upward to aid it in flight. As a flying machine it truly was a thing of beauty.

But it would not come into being.

We stood in the dark with the house blazing behind us as I focused on creating the flying machine.

Nothing happened.

'What's wrong?' Chad asked.

'It won't happen,' I said. 'I've been having some problems—'

'On the airplane,' his eyes shone with realization. 'When the bomb exploded—'

'I couldn't create a shield,' I admitted. 'I don't know what's wrong.'

'Could you have told us?' he asked angrily. 'You've put all of our lives at risk.'

'There hasn't been time—'

'Forget it!' he snapped. 'We've got to go the old fashioned way.'

'You mean—'

Moments later we were in the campervan barreling down the road. We reached the highway. The night was still and dark. I saw an animal scurry off into the roadside scrub. A car drove past us. Probably some late night partygoer from the city.

Far away in the distance we saw a vehicle moving away from us at high speed. It turned off and changed direction.

'Where does that road lead?' I asked.

'I don't know,' Chad said. 'I think there are some abandoned properties down there.'

'There are.' I remembered. On occasion I had flown around this area early in the morning before people were out of bed. There was an abandoned homestead and airfield. It had not been used for years. 'They must be taking them by plane somewhere.'

'Are you sure?'

'No,' I said truthfully. 'But using a plane would be the fastest way to escape.'

'Okay.' Chad pushed his foot down even harder on the accelerator. 'We'll do it your way.'

We sped through the darkness in silence. One part of me was worried about what might be happening to the others. The other part of me wondered how all this came into being. And then there was the whole business about the vampires.

Vampires were real. Really real. How had they survived all these centuries without being discovered? And who had planned this? And what on earth would a bunch of vampires want with a group of super powered kids?

Chad turned off onto the side road and now he increased speed again. The vehicle was bouncing badly all over the road. A hub cap flew off one of the campervan's wheels. We were moving at a terrible speed. He needed to slow down otherwise we wouldn't survive the car journey.

'We need to slow down,' I yelled.

'Do I tell you how to drive?' he yelled back angrily.

'No, but—'

I spotted a row of lights in the night. As we came up over the crest of a hill I realized we could see the takeoff lights for the airfield. A plane—some sort of cargo plane—was starting to taxi down the runway.

'There it is!' I yelled.

'I see it!'

Chad braked. Swerved. Accelerated again. The campervan hit a dip in the road and flew straight up into the air. It hit the road again. I heard something snap on the underneath of the vehicle. Somehow it kept moving.

The transport was directly ahead of us, but accelerating away at high speed. Chad slammed his foot down on the accelerator and we tore down the runway after it. I glanced over at him. If I'd known he was such a good driver I would have let him take the wheel more often.

We were getting close now. Fifty feet. Twenty feet.

'What're you going to do?' I yelled.

'Ram it!' he yelled back.

'What?'

He shot me a look. 'We've got to stop it now or we never will!'

He seemed to urge one last piece of energy out of the van and it accelerated again. We drew ever closer to the tail of the transport. A couple more feet. Ten feet. Five feet. I gripped the door and waited for the collision.

It never happened.

The plane lifted into the air, out of reach and began to rise up into the night.

'No!' I screamed.

Leaning out of the window, I focused on creating my flying platform and then in the dim headlights of the campervan, I saw it form next to the vehicle. Drawing back, I pushed the door open.

'What are you doing?' Chad asked.

'My powers are working again!' I said. 'I'm going after them.'

'Not without me!' he said.

I leapt through the door of the campervan and landed nimbly on the invisible platform. Whatever had gone wrong with my powers before had subsided. They were as good as ever. I steadied myself on the flying wing.

'Hey!' Chad's voice came from behind me.

I turned around just in time to see him leap from the door of the vehicle. I caught him nimbly on the edge of the wing. Our van—our beloved campervan—skidded sideways, hit a ditch and flipped over the road. It burst into flames as we soared up into the sky.

'Are you insane?' I asked.

Chad could have been killed. There were a dozen things that could have gone wrong. My powers could have failed again. He might not have landed on the wing. The van could have flipped before he had a chance to make the jump.

'You think I'm letting you have all the fun?'

he asked.

Fun? This is fun?

We rose higher into the sky. Within seconds we had caught up to the transport. It was only a matter of time now. We drew close to the side of the plane. I focused on forcing the side door open. Raising a shield, we landed nimbly inside. The interior of the aircraft was eerily silent after the racket of riding in the van and the ascent into the sky.

We slowly made our way up the center aisle of the aircraft.

The interior was empty. Stripped of all seating. Even the lighting had been removed from the ceiling. Chad looked at me in confusion. We arrived at the flight cabin and pulled open the door to confront the crew.

Instead, all we saw was a computer automated system. The flight cabin, like the rest of the plane, was empty.

No sooner had I realized this than the bomb located in the hull of the aircraft exploded, ripping the aircraft apart into a thousand pieces.

Chapter Twelve

Brodie awoke to find a trail of drool running down her chin. She wiped at it absently as she wondered about her alarm clock. Had Chad stolen it again? He had done it three times this week already. He was such a practical joker. Once she had awoken to find it snowing in her bedroom and Chad standing in the doorway laughing his head off. He thought he was so funny, but mostly he was just a pain in the ass.

Now she realized the rest of the furniture in her room was also gone. For some strange reason, she was lying on a camping bed. It was the type the army used for long term outdoor engagements. The rest of the room was empty apart from two other camping beds currently occupied by Ebony and Dan. The walls of this room were made from concrete. The door was metal.

The events of the previous day came rushing back to her.

Holy hell, she realized. *We've been kidnapped.*

For one long moment Brodie thought they had

been taken by The Agency, but she quickly dismissed the thought. This didn't seem like The Agency's style. And then there was a strange symbol on the door. It looked like a rifle superimposed over an image of the planet. Brodie had never seen it before, but it looked too militaristic for The Agency.

So who had kidnapped them? Vampires. She remembered the comment that Mr. Jones had made when he visited.

'Staying out of sight has kept mods alive for centuries...Mods are humans that have been modified...'

So vampires were a type of mod that had stayed hidden for centuries. Did that mean werewolves and ghouls and other creatures of the night were also a reality?

She shook her head.

Impossible.

But she had super powers and that was possible.

So vampires were real.

But what would they want with a bunch of

super-powered kids?

A sound came from the door. She noticed there was a slot at the bottom and it now slid up slightly and a tray appeared. It appeared to have sandwiches and a squat pitcher of water on it. As she went over to retrieve it, a tiny eye slot moved across at eye level.

'There's some food and water,' a voice said. 'I'd advise you to accept it gratefully and not cause any trouble.'

The voice sounded young. She wondered if it was one of the vampires.

'Why have we been brought here?' she asked.

'All that will be explained later,' the voice said. 'Just be grateful you are here.'

Be grateful—?

Brodie had never felt less grateful in her entire life.

'You have a strange way of treating your guests,' Brodie said. 'Attacking them. Kidnapping them. Holding them prisoner.'

She looked through the slot and saw the eye

was blue. It appeared to be a boy aged seventeen or eighteen.

'Are you a vampire?' she asked.

'Me?' The boy reacted in surprise. 'No! I'm not one of those freaks.'

'Then why are you working with them?'

'We're not.' The boy paused. 'Anyway, I can't talk to you. Not yet. Not until you've had everything properly explained. Until you fully understand.'

Brodie doubted she would ever fully understand or excuse what had been done to them. Still, now was not the time to debate it. Food and water had arrived and the first rule of survival was—survive!

'It's not poisoned,' she asked. 'Is it?'

'Hell, no,' the voice said in surprise. 'We don't want to hurt you, but there's something I want you to promise.'

'What's that?'

'Don't try to escape,' he said. 'I know you have powers, but do not try to escape.'

Brodie said nothing.

'Can you promise?' the boy asked.

'What's your name?'

'You have to promise.'

'I don't make the decisions,' Brodie said. 'I'm here with my friends.' A groan came from behind her. 'It sounds like one of them is waking up.'

'Jason,' the boy said. 'My name is Jason.'

'Thank you for the food and water, Jason,' Brodie said.

He did not reply. The eye slot slid back into position and Brodie picked up the tray. It was Ebony who was slowly coming to life. She was rubbing her head and wincing at the light. She sat up.

'How do you feel?' Brodie asked.

'Like death,' she groaned. 'Which is probably not too surprising considering a vampire tried to make me his eternal beloved.'

'Now that's doubly weird.'

'What is?'

'I think that's the longest sentence you've ever said.'

'I don't usually have anything to say.' Ebony looked at the food on the table. 'Is that what I think it is?'

'Not if you think it's a Big Mac and fries,' Brodie said. 'It's sandwiches and water.'

Ebony half stumbled when she tried to stand. Brodie grabbed her, directed her into a seat and poured her a glass of water.

'You don't look great,' Brodie said.

'I don't feel great. I think I might vomit.'

Brodie patted her shoulder sympathetically. Usually Ebony was not her favorite person. More than once she had noticed the quiet girl giving Axel glances out of the corner of her eye. The glances had made her feel...uneasy. Especially when he had looked up unexpectedly and smiled back at her.

She shouldn't be so jealous. She didn't own Axel. She couldn't control who he looked at or who looked at him. Despite sharing a few kisses over the last few months, they were not an item. She wasn't sure why not. He seemed to like her. She just assumed it had just been such a crazy time that relationships had to be put on the back burner.

Chad had certainly shown a lot more interest than Axel. When she thought about him she wondered if she could ever be in a relationship with the blonde headed boy. Chad was an egotistical show off and loud mouth. He was also very good looking.

Before Brodie could continue this line of thinking, Ebony suddenly pitched forward and vomited over the tray.

'Oh hell,' Brodie muttered.

As Ebony emptied the contents of her stomach, Brodie looked around for something to wipe her mouth. She finally picked up a cloth napkin and gave it to the girl. Ebony accepted it gratefully.

'Thanks,' she said. 'I think I'm feeling a little better now.'

'Wash your mouth out with water,' Brodie said. 'There's a small sink over here.'

As Ebony cleaned up, Brodie glanced over at Dan. He could sleep through a tornado, that kid. She focused on his face. Not only was he dead to the world, but he looked quite pale. She quickly felt his forehead and took his pulse.

Brodie turned to Ebony in shock. 'Something's wrong with Dan! He's barely breathing!'

Chapter Thirteen

There are times when you're lucky and there's times when you're unlucky. As the bomb exploded in the plane I was able to throw a shield around ourselves. It shielded us from the bulk of the blast. I then converted it into a flying wing and took us safely to earth.

I don't want to think about the other possibilities; that my powers could have failed at the moment the bomb exploded and we were blown to pieces. Or that my flying platform could have evaporated when we were halfway back to earth and we fell thousands of feet to the earth below, ending up as two bloody smears on the desert surface.

Like I said, best not to think of those possibilities.

It was bad enough that my powers failed again once we had landed, leaving us to walk back to civilization through the heart of the desert with the early morning sun beating down on our heads. Try doing that when you don't have food, water or a hat.

'So what's going on with your powers?' Chad asked after a few hours of marching across the same repetitive landscape. 'What's with the on/off switch?'

'I wish I knew,' I said.

I explained about the problems back on the plane and then back at the house. Normally Chad had a smart ass remark for everything, but this time he surprised me.

'What do you think is causing it?' he asked.

'I've got no idea.' We trudged over a rise in the landscape. 'Maybe it's the injections that caused our powers in the first place. Whoever said they were permanent?'

'No-one, I suppose,' Chad said. 'Is that a road up ahead?'

I could have jumped for joy. 'It is. I think it's the Ninety-Five.'

A truck moving across the landscape proved me right. It was US Route 95. Once I had thought of it as just another road. Now I felt like building a monument to its glory and writing a song in its praise. As we stomped across the sandy dirt toward it, I began to wonder about our next step.

Unless Brodie and the others had made a miraculous escape from their captors, they were still missing in action. The most logical plan would be for Chad and me to return home and make our plans from there. Except our home had been fully alight when we last saw it.

By the time we reached the highway, we must have been looking pretty bad. Usually Chad was impeccable about his appearance, but even he looked like he'd been living on the streets for six months. Several more hours of walking took us back to our house. Or what remained of it. It looked like both the fire brigade and the police had been here. What wasn't burnt had been ruined by the attempts by the fire brigade to extinguish the blaze. An untidy trail of police tape ran about the circumference of the property.

Chad and I barely said anything to each other. It was obvious the others were gone. They had not made a miraculous escape otherwise they would be here waiting for us. Chad and I trudged back to the highway. Fortunately this time a passing trucker took pity on us and gave us a ride.

'How did you boys end up all the way out here?' he asked.

'Our car broke down,' I explained.

'Where do you need to go?'

'Into Vegas,' I said, before Chad could reply. 'All the way into the city.'

Chad shot me a look, but I gave him a look.

Later.

The driver dropped us off on South Las Vegas Boulevard and we gave him a cheery wave goodbye.

'Do you mind telling me what we're doing here?' Chad asked.

'We need help if we're going to find the others.'

'What sort of help?'

'Agency kind of help.'

'Are you insane?' he asked. 'We wouldn't be in this situation if it weren't for those crazies!'

Actually, he was kind of right in saying that. If The Agency hadn't pumped us full of drugs and given us super powers we probably wouldn't be standing on South Las Vegas Boulevard with no money, no identification and no memory of our previous lives.

Life's funny like that.

I even told him so.

Chad looked like he wanted to hit me. 'I'm not contacting The Agency. I'm not going back there. I'm going back to the house and taking my life back.'

'What life?' I was starting to get annoyed now. 'And what house? It's a smoldering wreck in the middle of the desert!'

That shut him up. Even in his desert addled, water deprived state of mind he could see my logic.

'So how will we contact The Agency?' he asked.

I reached into my pocket and produced a card that Mr. Jones had given me the previous day.

'I have an address.'

Chad shook his head. 'This is a mistake.'

'Do you have a better idea?'

He didn't.

Cars whizzed by at great speeds as we

marched down the road. I reflected how this whole area must have changed over the years. A century ago American Indians would have hunted and gathered as they had for thousands of years. Now the same territory had been eaten up by wedding chapels, bail bondsman, pawn stores, restaurants and low rise hotels.

Who would have thought it?

We finally arrived at the address on the card. I looked down at the address and double checked it. Yep, this was the place.

It was not quite what I expected.

'The Hound Dog Wedding Chapel?' Chad read the sign in disbelief. 'Are you sure this is the right place?'

'This is it.' I started up the path. 'Let's see if Elvis is home.'

Chapter Fourteen

'We need help!' Brodie hammered the metal door. 'Our friend is unwell!'

She had been hitting the door for a full minute by the time a female voice replied from the other side.

'That's the oldest trick in the book,' the voice said. 'We weren't born yesterday.'

'It's not a trick!' Brodie yelled. 'Besides, if we wanted to be out of here, we would be.'

'We know you have some crazy powers,' the woman replied. She sounded older than the teenage boy with whom Brodie had spoken. 'I advise you to just eat your food and settle in. Tomorrow morning we can—'

'My friend might not last till tomorrow!' Brodie snapped. 'Ebony!'

Ebony knew exactly what to do. Dan's breathing was dangerously shallow. He could die if they didn't take some proactive measures. She crossed to the metal door and touched it with her bare hand.

'Oxygen,' she said.

The door transmuted into oxygen, revealing a surprised woman on the other side. She was dressed in army fatigues and carrying a rifle. She started to raise the weapon. Brodie leapt forward, grabbed the weapon and twisted it one hundred and eighty degrees out of her grasp.

She pointed it at the astonished woman. Looking left and right, she realized she was in a long concrete passageway leading in both directions. She could take this woman hostage, but she had no idea where the exit was from this place. In addition, she wasn't sure they could carry Dan with them all the way.

Plus they still had to find Ferdy.

At that moment a door opened at the other end of the passageway. A good looking young man appeared. Brodie thought it was Jason.

He raised his rifle and pointed it at her. 'Put that gun down!'

'Listen to me—' Brodie began.

'Put it down!'

'My friend is sick!' Brodie snapped. 'He's not breathing properly. He needs medical assistance.'

'I don't believe you,' the youth said.

Brodie was exasperated. 'What is it with you people? You have to believe me!'

'Do you have a doctor?' Ebony asked.

'Yes, but—'

'As a symbol of good faith, my friend will put her weapon down,' Ebony said.

Brodie felt none too happy with complying with the idea, but she could see the sense in it. 'We will not attack you,' she said. 'All we want is help for our friend.'

Brodie placed the gun down. If the young man decided to shoot her, she doubted she could dodge out of the way in time.

'Get your gun, Donna,' the youth said.

The woman named Donna scooped up the weapon. 'She's fast, Jason. Watch out for her.'

Ebony stepped into the corridor. 'Dan's getting worse. He needs help.'

Jason pointed them back into the room with

his rifle. Donna looked down at his inert form.

'He doesn't look well,' she peered down at him.

'That's what we've been trying to tell you,' Brodie said. 'Do you have a doctor?'

'Doc Williams can look at him,' Donna said. 'You young people better not be trying anything—'

'We're not,' Ebony said. 'We just want help for our friend.'

'I'll get the doc,' Donna said, departing the room.

Brodie found herself clenching her teeth in annoyance. Hopefully this doctor had some sort of proper qualifications, otherwise she and Ebony would have to fight their way out of here. Jason kept his gun trained on them until they heard the sound of a door opening and closing.

Donna returned with a man who was aged about sixty. He wore military fatigues like the others, but he had a red cross sewn onto his pocket and carried a leather medical bag. Kneeling down beside Dan, he quickly took his pulse and checked his breathing. After a moment he pulled out a small bottle and needle from his bag.

'What's that?' Brodie asked in alarm.

'Don't panic, missy,' he said. 'Your friend's had an allergic reaction to the hypodermic. I'm just giving him something to ease his breathing. He'll be back to new before you know it.'

He injected Dan. Almost immediately, the boy's color seemed to improve as did his breathing. It did not sound so labored. Brodie gave the doctor a grateful look.

'Thank you for your help,' she said.

'That's okay,' he said. 'It's my job.'

'When can we get out of here?' Ebony had sat back down on her bunk bed. 'Why have we been taken prisoner?'

The doctor held up a hand. 'It's not my place to answer those kinds of questions, but a man will be here shortly who will set your minds at ease.'

I doubt that, Brodie thought. *The only thing that will set my mind at ease will be leaving this place.*

As the doctor exited, Donna and Jason hovered in the entryway where the metal door used to be. They gave the gap a critical look.

'We won't try to escape,' Brodie said. 'You have my word.'

Jason seemed satisfied, but Donna looked undecided.

'We're not leaving our friend,' Ebony said. 'And he obviously can't travel so it looks like we're stuck here whether we like it or not.'

Donna nodded and departed. Jason gave them an appraising look.

'You people have got powers,' he said. 'That's going to come in handy.'

'Why?' Brodie asked.

'You'll see,' he said enigmatically.

They heard the door open down the passage and a man sidled past Jason into the room. He was completely bald. Even apart from his baldness, Brodie realized he looked unusual and it took her a few seconds to work out why.

Oh my God, she thought.

He had no ears.

'My name is Jeremiah Stead,' he said in a deep, confident voice. 'I'm in charge here.'

'Where is 'here'?' Brodie asked. 'Exactly.'

'You're at the Sanctuary Compound in Montana,' he said. 'Consider yourselves to be among the fortunate few.'

'What do you mean?' Ebony asked.

Jeremiah smiled grimly and gave them a wink. 'The world is coming to an end,' he said. 'It's your lucky day, kids.'

Chapter Fifteen

I stopped at the front steps of the Hound Dog Wedding Chapel. It was a two story cream colored stucco building with a small bell tower and signage on the front indicating a selection of various wedding packages. They ranged from a traditional service conducted by a certified minister to the full performance where you could be married by a rock n roll singing and dancing Elvis.

Wow, I thought. *If Brodie and I ever decide to tie the knot...*

A Chinese restaurant sat to one side of the building. On the other was a small hotel. They even had deals where you could combine a three day weekend package with a complimentary Elvis wedding.

'This is too weird,' Chad moaned. 'How did it all come to this?'

'Do you really want an answer to that?'

'No.'

We rung the front bell and it chimed a little

ditty for a few seconds. I thought it may have been Can't Help Falling In Love by Elvis. The door opened and the King of Rock and Roll—or a fairly reasonable facsimile—stood in the entrance. He was wearing a white jumpsuit with a bright red collar and flared pants. The entire outfit was decorated with gold grommets and colored rhinestones.

'Hello boys,' he said. 'Lookin' to get hitched?'

'Not to each other!' Chad exclaimed.

'I have a card,' I said. 'I'm here to see Mr. Floyd.'

Elvis nodded. 'Come right in boys. You've arrived at the right place.'

He opened the door wide and we stepped inside. We found ourselves in a short corridor. The walls were painted lilac pink. The interior smelt of cologne. Plastic flowers decorated the corners. Pictures of Elvis decorated the walls as well as dozens of photos of newlywed couples.

'I'm in Hell,' Chad muttered.

Elvis ignored him. 'Come on through to the

chapel, boys.'

We followed him into a clean and neat chamber with rows of seating on both sides. A small enclosed gazebo sat at the front. Its ceiling was made of hanging pink satin sheets and plastic white and pink roses. An organ was located to the left of the gazebo. An elderly lady was practicing the organ.

She looked up at us. 'Hello boys.'

'Ma'am,' I greeted her.

'They're looking for Mr. Floyd,' Elvis said.

She nodded.

Elvis hit a button on the left hand side of the gazebo. There was a soft click and the entire structure lifted up into the ceiling. Directly below it was a small and modern looking elevator enclosed in steel and dark glass.

'Mr. Floyd is right this way,' Elvis said.

We wordlessly stepped into the elevator.

Elvis winked. 'If you rethink that marriage…'

Doors slid across and Chad and I looked at each other. Before we could say a word we felt the elevator smoothly drop a few feet. The doors slid open. A modern office lay before us. We could see about twenty desks with people working at wide screen computers.

We stepped out of the elevator. On both the left and right of the chamber were walls with various maps of parts of the world displayed on them. Military personnel were all over the place, speaking to administrative employees.

A woman aged about twenty-five with short black hair and round rimmed glasses suddenly appeared. She wore a neat, blue office suit and flat shoes.

'You are looking for Mr. Floyd?' she said. 'Your names are—?'

'Axel,' I said. 'And Chad.'

She nodded. 'Follow me.'

Leading us through the heart of the office, we reached a barrier and I abruptly realized the entire office was actually only a mezzanine area. Beyond it lay an even larger room, hundreds of feet in length. At the far end lay a massive video display made up of small screened television sets. There seemed to be hundreds of different channels playing at once. Hundreds of other desks had people sitting at them, typing or speaking over hands free phones.

'Wow,' said Chad.

'You're right about that,' I replied. 'Super-wow.'

A man weaved his way through the maze of desks toward us. He was tall, clean shaven with short cropped brown hair, a gray suit and shiny black shoes.

'Hello boys,' he greeted us. 'I'm Mr. Floyd.'

We introduced ourselves.

'Mr. Jones told me you might be in contact with us,' he said. 'I'm glad you took the initiative.'

'Actually the initiative was taken away from us,' I said. 'We were attacked last night by—'

He held up a hand. 'Let's find a meeting room first.'

We followed him in silence past the back wall with all the television screens. Beyond it lay another sunken area where more people were working at desks inputting information and speaking on phones.

My mind was whirling. All of this was taking place beneath Las Vegas. In fact, it was taking place directly underneath the Hound Dog Wedding Chapel. I was dying to ask him about the installation, but now was not the time. He led us into a meeting room with a large oval desk surrounded by about twenty chairs. A screen hung from the wall at the front of the desk. Mr. Floyd indicated chairs to us while the girl in the suit closed the door behind us.

'I don't know if you've been introduced to Agent Palmer,' Mr. Floyd said.

We nodded greetings to her.

'Okay boys,' Mr. Floyd. 'Tell it from the top.'

Between the two of us, we spent the next fifteen minutes describing the events of the last twenty-four hours. Chad even brought my fading super powers into the discussion which I wished he had kept to himself. Finally we told them about making our way back into town and arriving at the Hound Dog Wedding Chapel.

Mr. Floyd nodded. 'Okay,' he said. 'Let's get the bad news out of the way first. We picked up a news story earlier about your house in the desert. The fire department was called out there after motorists on the interstate saw a glow in the sky.

'They found the whole place had burnt to the ground with nothing left standing.' He paused. 'Regarding your powers, Axel, I'm not sure what to make of that. I know very little about The Alpha Project. Are there any scientists remaining from the original program?'

I was surprised. I expected him to know more than me. 'I don't know,' I said. 'I don't think so. I think they were killed and the research destroyed.'

He thought for a moment. 'Twelve's actions are infamous. He brought an enormous amount of disrepute to The Agency.'

Chad and I didn't say anything in response to this.

Mr. Floyd continued. 'I do have some thoughts about the group that attacked you. From your descriptions they sound like a group of vampires that call themselves Wormwood. They've been working this part of the country for decades.'

'Vampires,' Chad repeated the word as if Mr. Floyd had said something in a foreign language. 'We are talking real vampires.'

'Of course,' he confirmed. 'Vampires have existed for centuries. They prospered until Bram Stoker wrote Dracula. When that book was released they realized they had to revert to a low profile. They've remained underground while the view of their fictional selves has propagated.'

'What would they want with Brodie and the others?' I asked.

'Nothing,' Mr. Floyd said. 'Wormwood are a type of bounty hunter. People pay them to carry out tasks and duties like a Special Forces team. They would have been under the employ of someone else.'

'So this someone else is the one pulling the strings,' I said.

'Exactly,' Mr. Floyd replied.

'So where do we go from here?' Chad asked. 'We need to get our friends back.'

'And we want to help you,' Mr. Floyd said. 'But we are going to need an assurance from you.'

'What sort of assurance?' I asked.

'That you are prepared to be affiliated with The Agency,' he said. 'We need—'

'No way,' Chad interrupted. 'I am not working for you people. Especially after what you did to us.'

Mr. Floyd held up his hand. 'Please hear me out. Try to think of the arrangement as being, not so much working for The Agency, but working with The Agency. We have mutual aims. You want your people back. We want them safe too.'

'What's your interest in this?' I asked suspiciously.

'There is a change in the air,' Mr. Floyd. 'I can't say what that is, but I can tell you this. Some time soon you'll have to make up your mind as to whose side you're on.'

'What sort of change?' I asked.

'We're not at liberty to say,' Agent Palmer said. 'All we can say is that a big change is coming. Whether you like it or not, you're going to be part of that change. We are prepared to help you get your friends back, but we need you to be on side for us too.'

'I can't speak for the others—' I began.

'I don't expect you to,' Mr. Floyd said. 'But you can speak for yourselves. We want you onside after all this is over. If you can't agree to that then…' He shrugged.

'Then what?' Chad asked.

Mr. Floyd inclined his head. 'The door is that way.'

I took a deep breath and let it out slowly. We were being offered a way forward, a way to help our friends, but there was a cost. I wondered about the alternatives. We had no money. No home. No car. Nothing. Only the clothes on our backs. The Agency could change all that.

Chad seemed to be having the same thoughts. He looked across at me glumly. I know he hated the idea, but there was little else we could do. Chad might happily abandon me and Dan and the others, but Ebony was his sister. He would not leave her in a million years.

'Okay,' he said. 'Count me in.'

'Me too,' I said.

Agent Palmer nodded. 'There are some details we need to work out. We will be supplying standard contracts to you—'

'Contracts?' I interrupted.

'—but we don't need to worry about those yet,' she concluded. 'First of all we need to find your friends. The paperwork can come later.'

'In the meantime,' Mr. Floyd said, 'you boys need some food and sleep. We'll get someone to show you to a room. Hopefully we'll have a lead for you by morning.'

Both Mr. Floyd and Agent Palmer left the chamber. I was slightly relieved to note that the door closed, but was not locked after their departure. Chad looked over at me and slowly shook his head.

'It looks like we're back,' he said. 'For better—'

'—or for worse.'

I hoped it was the former and not the latter.

Chapter Sixteen

'The good news is we believe your friends are alive and well,' Mr. Floyd began. 'The bad news is we think they're being held by a man named Jeremiah Stead.'

It was the next day. We were sitting in a meeting room in another part of The Agency complex beneath the streets of Las Vegas. Our new residence was a room in a hotel called The Windsor Arms. It was located down the block from The Hound Dog Wedding Chapel. I don't know what they told regular people who wanted to stay in the hotel, but as far as we could tell, the entire place was reserved strictly for Agency personnel.

Our room was on the third floor and had a view across the Western side of Las Vegas across the great urban sprawl. It wasn't the greatest view, but we weren't there to look out the window.

Agent Palmer had collected us before eight o'clock and taken us to a cafeteria in the hotel. After that she took us down an elevator and through a labyrinth of corridors to a meeting room where Mr. Floyd was already waiting for us.

'Who is Jeremiah Stead?' I asked.

'I believe you've already had a discussion about him with Mr. Jones,' Mr. Floyd said.

I looked at him blankly.

'Jeremiah Stead is the man responsible for the theft of the Doomsday virus from the Germans,' Mr. Floyd explained. 'Possibly that rings a bell.'

More than a bell. Rather, it rang a long and disturbing chime of doom.

'How does all this fit together?' Chad asked.

'You may have heard of the rise of militia groups in the United States over recent years,' Mr. Floyd said. 'They are isolated groups, very often numbering less than a few dozen individuals who band together against the government.'

'Why are they against the government?' I asked.

'They generally share a belief that the government is working against them and they have to take up arms to protect themselves.'

'Where would they get that idea?' Chad asked sarcastically.

Mr. Floyd ignored him. 'Most of these groups are harmless, although a number of them have turned to violence over the years. As they break laws the government is required to step in and bring them to justice.'

'I saw something on television about the Freeman movement,' I said.

Mr. Floyd nodded. 'They were one of the more violent groups. There have been others. Confrontations between the FBI and these groups have resulted in shoot outs and deaths.'

'I still don't see what this has to do with Ebony and the others,' Chad said.

'We believe that your sister and the others were collateral damage,' Agent Palmer said. 'We think your friend Ferdy was their real target.'

'Ferdy?' Chad said in disbelief. 'He can barely tie his shoelace. Why would they want him?'

'Ferdy is challenged,' Agent Palmer agreed. 'But he is far from stupid. Prior to leaving The

Agency his IQ was measured to be three hundred and ten.'

'Three hundred and ten?' I said. 'Isn't the average around one hundred?'

'It is indeed,' Mr. Floyd confirmed. 'Ferdy not only has a staggering ability to remember information, but he also has a unique ability to work with numbers and patterns.'

I was finding this a little hard to believe. We had grown to accept Ferdy as one of our group over the last few months. Particularly since he had been so badly treated by The Agency, we had made a point of making certain he felt like an integral part of our dysfunctional family. In that time, however, apart from his amazing abilities to single-handedly wipe the Trivial Pursuit board with us or throw a car thirty feet, he had displayed little in the way of survival skills.

He could barely change channels on the television without our help and Chad's comment about his inability to tie his shoelace was not far off the mark. I had persevered in helping him carry out normal day to day tasks, but it had been a long battle. I had seen improvements, but it had made me sometimes wonder if he wouldn't be better off in some sort of institution.

An IQ of three hundred and ten?

Really?

'Assuming you're right,' I said. 'How can Ferdy help them?'

Agent Palmer continued. 'Doomsday is sealed within a tube constructed from T5K. That's an incredibly dense metal only recently developed by the British government. It's unlikely that even a nuclear blast could break it open.

'A sophisticated locking mechanism keeps Doomsday contained. The code that operates that mechanism is called Barricade. It has some two hundred billion unique combinations. We believe it's unbreakable, even by the world's most sophisticated system.'

'But if a computer can't break it—' Chad started.

'How can a human?' Agent Palmer asked.

'The human brain has between eighty and one hundred and twenty billion neurons. For most of us those neurons are sitting dormant while we carry out important duties like watching TV or eating our meals.

'Ferdy's brain is differently wired. He is able to focus his brain solely on a problem until he comes up with a solution. He is able to examine a problem from both a human and computer perspective. He can make leaps in thinking beyond any computer. He can see patterns to which the rest of us are blind.'

'So you think Ferdy can crack this code?' I asked.

'We think he can,' Mr. Floyd confirmed. 'Apparently, so does Jeremiah Stead.'

'So where is Stead?' I asked. 'And where are our friends?'

'We believe they are holed up in a place they call Sanctuary Compound. It's located somewhere in Montana, but we don't know its exact location.' Mr. Floyd paused. 'We believe they will use Ferdy to break Barricade's encryption and release Doomsday into the environment.'

'So how do we find out the location of the compound?' Chad asked.

'Jeremiah Stead's brother—Zachary—is being held by the North Koreans in a jail known as Yodak. The jail contains two types of prisoners—humans and mods. We believe the North Koreans will agree to a prisoner exchange. While they would not agree to release Zachary, we believe they will accept two mods in exchange for two human Americans being held at the jail.

'We think they will see the deal as being highly advantageous to them. So advantageous they cannot possibly say no.'

'What mods are you—' I started.

Of course.

Us.

'The mods would be you and Chad,' Agent Palmer said. 'Once within Yodak you would need to make contact with Zachary and then break out. Upon reaching the coast, you can make use of a vessel to enable your escape from North Korea.

'Obviously you must appear to be operating independently of The Agency to gain Zachary Stead's trust. As long as you espouse similar sentiments, we believe he will lead you straight to the Compound.'

'I've just one question,' Chad said. 'This Yodak jail. Has anyone ever escaped from it?'

'No,' Mr. Floyd said. 'But there's a first time for everything.'

Chapter Seventeen

Brodie was relieved to see that conditions had relaxed enough to allow her and Ebony to leave their cell and join the main population of the Sanctuary Compound. Dan was still recovering from his illness and remained in his bunk. At least his condition was improving since the doctor's ministrations.

Jeremiah Stead had told them the previous day that they could mingle with the other people in the compound as long as they did not try to cause any violence.

Brodie thought that was laughable considering they were the ones who had been kidnapped.

'What's to stop us from leaving?' Brodie asked.

'Nothing,' Jeremiah said. 'But then I would be forced to take measures against your friends Dan and Ferdy.'

'What kind of measures?' she asked.

'Extreme measures.'

Whatever that meant.

The Sanctuary complex turned out to be a concrete structure buried under the earth among a forest of spruce trees. There appeared to be only one exit point and even this was hidden under an overhang of foliage. Brodie doubted it could ever be seen from the air.

They were allowed outside of the bunker. It was autumn and the weather was starting to turn cold, but Brodie didn't mind. They had spent two days underground and fresh air was almost as welcome as freedom.

While it was impossible to determine the size of the structure, there were clearly a lot of people living in the building. Almost two hundred including children, she estimated. How they had ever built the structure in the first place was beyond her.

Jason was quite enthusiastic in how well they hid their operations. Some distance away there was a camp above ground inhabited by another twenty or so people.

'That's so we can get supplies delivered,' he explained. 'But the suppliers don't speak to each other so they don't know how much really gets delivered.'

'Sounds like you've got everything worked out,' she said without enthusiasm.

'My father is a brilliant man,' Jason said.

'Your father?'

'Jeremiah Stead,' he said.

Brodie could hardly keep the expression of amazement from her face. 'And your father is convinced the end of the world is coming?'

'Absolutely.'

'What makes you so sure he's correct?'

'He has studied hundreds of books about the end times,' Jason said. 'He prophesized the rise of The New World Order and now that prophecy is coming to pass.'

'Who is the New World Order?' Ebony asked.

'It's an organization controlled by the United Nations,' Jason said. 'The NWO is designed to create a single, one world government. No person who loves liberty could stand for such a thing.'

'I don't really know anything about it,' Brodie

said.

'I'll teach you. You'll need to know anyway because you'll be staying here.'

Brodie shot Ebony a look and they didn't reply.

Temporary breakfast tables with seating were lined up under the spruce trees. Bowls were filled with serves of porridge and plastic cups containing orange cordial were passed out to everyone.

It was all very efficient, Brodie noted. Whatever could be said for these wacko people, they were good at what they did.

It was a shame they were so misguided.

After breakfast the plastic crockery was collected up, the tables dismantled and everything taken back inside. A woman came up to them as the various members went in their different directions.

'My name is Susan,' she said. 'Jeremiah has told me you're welcome to walk around out here just as long as you don't cause trouble.'

Brodie was getting a bit sick of this line about trouble.

'We won't cause any problems,' she said. 'Actually we're interested in seeing how things work around here.'

'I'll show you around,' Susan said.

'Thanks.'

Good, Brodie thought. *Information is power.*

The woman took them down to a nearby river and showed them how their water was transported up the hill. Essentially they used a bucket brigade in the early morning that quickly moved enormous amounts in a very short time.

'Isn't there machinery that can do this?' Ebony asked.

'Machinery takes fuel,' Susan said. 'There's no guarantee there'll be any fuel when the End Times arrive.'

'How do you know the End Times are coming?' Brodie asked.

'Jeremiah has told us,' Susan said. 'He knows these things.'

'But Jeremiah could be wrong,' Brodie said.

Susan smiled. 'He's not wrong about this. The

UN has been secretly pulling the strings behind governments for years. They have even pushed for limits on worldwide population growth.'

'But surely that's because of the stress on the environment?' Brodie said.

'There are limited resources,' Susan said. 'No doubt about that, but they want to pick and choose who should receive those resources.' Susan's voice grew hard. 'No-one's telling me and my children we have no right to live.'

Brodie doubted the United Nations was actually doing that, but she didn't argue. Susan showed them small patches of potatoes, carrots and onions they were growing. The quantities seemed so insubstantial that Brodie doubted they would feed a population as large as the Sanctuary group for any lengthy period of time.

When she mentioned this to Susan, the woman merely nodded.

'These are just short term supplies,' she said. 'After the end times come the rest of humanity will be laid bare. There will be food enough for those who remain.'

'Jeremiah seems pretty certain the world is coming to an end,' Ebony said. 'In fact he said it's happening within the next week.'

'He has told us that,' Susan confirmed.

'And you believe him?' Ebony said.

'It's happening if Jeremiah says it's happening.'

What a dangerous way to be, Brodie thought. *It's like a kind of blindness.*

Susan slowly led them up the hill to the compound. The door to the structure was open. Brodie wanted to turn around and never return to this madhouse. She was sure Ebony felt the same way. It would be so easy to escape from this place, but they could not abandon Dan and Ferdy.

They followed Susan inside and back to the main hall. It was a single large chamber with posters around the walls talking about the New World Order and the End Times. Susan left them and returned to her regular duties—whatever they were—while Brodie and Ebony moved around the room reading the posters.

'This is crazy stuff,' Ebony said in a low voice.

'It's crazy,' Brodie agreed. 'But these people seem to believe it.'

'A lot of people do. I read an article in a magazine last month about the End Times. It said that about one in five Americans believe the end of the world will happen in their lifetimes.'

'It might be a type of wishful thinking,' Brodie suggested.

'What do you mean?'

'I think a similar thing happened at the outbreak of the First World War There were some people who believed the war would actually be a good thing.'

'Why would they believe such a thing?'

'They thought it would clear away all the old animosities and the world could start again from scratch,' Brodie explained. 'Sort of starting with a clean slate.'

'It didn't really work out that way.'

'Not really. Not with millions of people killed in the war.'

A man had been eyeing them from the other side of the room. He was a bookish looking figure with thick lens glasses and a crew cut. He sidled over to them and introduced himself as Ethan Craddock.

'Have you been here long?' Brodie asked.

'About six months.' He smiled pleasantly before glancing around. He seemed to make certain no-one was nearby. He lowered his voice. 'We need to talk.'

'About what?'

He didn't answer her question. 'There's an area behind the compound where we leave our garden scraps. Can we meet there in an hour?'

'Why?' Ebony asked.

'I'm an undercover operative with the FBI,' Ethan whispered. 'You cannot tell anyone or I'll be killed immediately.'

Brodie and Ebony looked at each other.

'Of course,' Brodie said. 'We'll keep it to—'

'Jeremiah is a dangerous individual,' Ethan

interrupted her. 'We need to get word out in relation to what's about to happen here.'

'You mean his End Times stuff?' Brodie asked. 'Surely that's all in his head.'

Ethan looked fearful. 'Not only is it real, but it's imminent. If Jeremiah has his way, this time next week most of the people on Earth will be dead.'

Chapter Eighteen

'North Korea has one of the most oppressive regimes in history,' Agent Palmer explained as the plane soared over the Sea of Japan. 'The country is held within a grip of secrecy and propaganda. Famine is common. Executions are rampant. Torture of prisoners is a common occurrence.'

'You really know how to sell a place.' I glanced out the window at the ocean below. 'Is there anything good about it at all?'

She ignored my question. 'We will be swapping you for two Americans held by the North Koreans for the last three years. After you extricate Zachary Stead from the compound we will have an invisible plane waiting for you on the coast. You'll need a transponder device to find it.'

We both stared at Agent Palmer.

'Invisible?' Chad was the first to speak. 'You've got to be kidding.'

'Not at all,' she said. 'The world is a strange place and you might as well get used to it.' She pulled two syringes from her jacket.

'What are they for?' I asked.

'I'll be injecting the transponders so the North Korean authorities won't detect them. After you leave the camp you follow the signal. You'll be able to see the plane, but no-one else will until you deactivate the invisibility shield.'

'How are we going to fly this thing?' I asked. 'Neither of us knows how to fly a plane.'

'It will fly itself. Once you climb aboard it has VTOL capabilities.'

'What's VTOL?' Chad asked.

'Vertical Take Off and Landing,' the agent explained. 'It is a ship, a plane and a submarine. It has an automatic guidance system that can take you anywhere you want. Hopefully that will be to a compound in Montana.'

'So why aren't we using it to go there?' Chad asked. 'If this super plane is so great.'

'It hasn't been properly tested,' Agent Palmer said. 'We at least wanted to get you this far safely.'

Great, I thought. *If we survive North Korea*

we'll end up on some sort of experimental jet that might just blow up with us on it.

This was all a bit too much. I knew our lives had turned upside down over the last few months, but this was sounding a whole lot like James Bond. I wondered if I should have worn a tuxedo.

'Do I get a code number?' I asked.

'A code number?'

'Yeah, like 007.'

'You have a code name.'

'What's that?'

'Axel.'

My name. All right. That would have to do.

'North Korea is a hostile place,' Agent Palmer said. 'You'll see things that will turn your stomach. Things that will make you sick. Just try to stay focused on your mission. You can't help anyone if you don't keep it together.'

'We can handle it,' Chad said, but he didn't look confident saying it.

The tone of the plane's engine changed. We would be jumping from the plane over the next few minutes to be picked up by North Korean forces. My heart was thudding in my chest. We had leapt from a plane before, but it was not an experience I relished.

I wondered about our missing friends, but mostly I wondered about Brodie. I hoped she was all right. My stomach jangled with tension every time I thought about her.

It had been three days since we had lost them. The longer they were missing, the greater the chance they would come to harm. It appeared the only person they really needed was Ferdy. It was terrible to think of Brodie and the others as simply being expendable.

'Three minutes till jump,' a military man yelled from the open doorway.

'One last thing,' Agent Palmer said. 'They know you are mods. You will encounter other mods at the jail. It might get hairy in there.'

'Hairy? What do you mean?' I asked.

'Jail is a tough place,' the agent said. 'You may have to prove yourselves.'

'Two minutes,' the military man yelled.

He and the agent did one last check of our

gear.

'I have a nephew your age,' Agent Palmer said. 'We shouldn't be sending kids like you out there.'

It was the closest any of The Agency employees had come to a sincere desire for our safety.

'We'll be okay,' I told her.

'All this is going to change soon,' she said enigmatically.

'What is?'

'One minute.'

There was no time for Agent Palmer to further elaborate. She simply pursed her lips and led us to the rear door of the aircraft. Seconds later we jumped, assuming the position we had been taught by Agency personnel. Below us lay the sea, a wide open shimmering planet of azure blue. The chutes opened normally and before long both Chad and I were floating gently toward the water.

It was only as we landed that I saw a naval ship approaching us flying a red, white and blue flag decorated with a single star. The ship pulled up alongside us and we were dragged aboard.

'Hey fellas!' Chad greeted them. 'Going our way?'

The soldiers glared at us.

'No sense of humor?' Chad asked.

The unsmiling military personnel silently handcuffed us with our hands in front and put us in a cabin below deck. I felt nervous. Chad still had his powers intact. Mine seemed to be in a state of flux, ready to turn on or off at any time.

'You're quiet,' Chad said.

'I'm worried.'

'No need to worry,' he said. 'I'm here.'

'That's one of the things I'm worried about.'

The ship pulled into a dock. A warm wind swept across us as we disembarked. The sky was overcast. It looked like rain. We were led up a pier toward a waiting truck and pushed into the back. The engine revved and the vehicle started. There were small windows on both sides of the truck so we stood up and gripped the bars. The vehicle trundled through a small village.

'Oh no,' I said softly.

Even Chad was speechless. We saw villagers walking past dressed in rags. They looked like they were starving. A dead body lay by the side of the road. It looked like they had been there for several days.

'What's going on?' Chad asked.

'Famine,' I explained. 'Like Agent Palmer said, this country is under the thumb of a brutal dictatorship. Add to that an embargo by the United Nations and this place is completely isolated from the rest of the world.'

It started to rain. A sweeping wind plastered the landscape with moisture. More bodies lay by the side of the road.

A huge complex lay at the end of the road. It had no windows. It almost looked like it was made from a single block of concrete. The only entrance to the place seemed to be a single gate guarded by half a dozen military personnel. The truck slowed down as the gate drew open. We entered an internal courtyard and drew to a halt. The gate closed.

The back door of the truck opened and Chad and I stepped out. We were surrounded by a dozen guards.

A door opened in the main building and a man walked down a short flight of stairs. He crossed the courtyard to where we were standing.

'My name is Ro Chin. I am the commander of this jail.' He grinned at us without a trace of humor. 'How is it you foreigners say it? Oh yes.' The smile fell from his lips.

'Welcome to Hell.'

Chapter Nineteen

'The American soldiers must have been most important to your government,' Ro said. 'They were of little assistance to us; the information they supplied was virtually useless.'

We said nothing.

'Your names have been supplied to me, as have your abilities,' he continued. 'Despite your talents, I assure you we can make your time here most unpleasant. If you follow the rules, you may survive. Yodak has a mortality rate of ninety percent, even for mods such as yourselves.

'Most of those deaths occur in the first year of incarceration before the inmate learns our rules.' He drew closer to us. 'Those rules are simple. We will not tolerate disobedience. You will follow our rules to the letter or you will pay the price.'

'I have a question,' Chad said.

'Yes?'

'Can you order takeout?'

The military commander drew a hand back

and slapped Chad across the face, knocking him to the ground. Chad's hands were still handcuffed behind his back. He looked so furious I thought he was about to make Ro Chin burst into flames. Somehow he kept his powers in check as two of the guards hoisted him to his feet.

'You have a sense of humor now,' Ro Chin said. 'We will see how your humor survives over the days, weeks and years that lie ahead.'

The commander turned his back and a group of soldiers led us across the small courtyard. Another gate opened. We passed through it into another courtyard; this one was larger and for the first time we could see the full extent of the jail. It was a massive facility with hundreds of tiny windows looking out onto the courtyard.

A long scream, terrifying and pitiful at the same time, rang out across the courtyard. It was impossible to tell from which of the many cells it originated. The cry finally ended and a helpless sobbing reverberated around the inner walls.

In the center of the courtyard lay a small

windowless cinder block building with a metal entry door. A soldier stood on each side of it. They opened the door wide and we were led down a flight of stairs. The door slammed shut behind us. Another set of doors lay before us. These were of the high tech variety and consisted of a retina scan. One of the guards placed his eye against the scanner and the door quietly clicked open.

We passed through this and descended down another flight of stairs. It had been warm above ground. Now it grew even hotter. We reached another set of doors. This was activated via a code entered into a keypad.

'You really don't want us to leave,' Chad said to one of the guards. 'Do you?'

'No-one has ever escaped Yodak Jail,' the man said.

'The accommodation's that good?'

'No-one has ever escaped,' the guard repeated.

The door opened and this time a hot fetid smell swept up from the steps below. Smoke filled the air. We descended the steps to the floor far below. At this level we could see the underground chamber had been divided into two main cells. Darkened alcoves containing men in rags lay along the rear of both sections. Many of the men were Caucasians. Some were Asian. Most of them had beards. Some of the men looked old and worn out, although I suspected their appearance, on closer inspection, could be mostly attributed to malnutrition rather than age.

A gate opened up and our cuffs were removed.

The same guard who had spoken to Chad relocked the gate.

'My name is Lee. You will deal mostly with me during your time here. The conditions here are harsh, but it is only what you deserve. You must be punished for your capitalist imperialist western notions. We are aware of your powers, but you will not use them against the guards.'

'I can't promise anything,' Chad said. 'I'm an impulsive kind of guy.'

'Your impulses will only cause you difficulty here,' Lee said. 'If you assault a guard we will not discipline you. We will discipline your fellow prisoners.'

He let this thought sink in. 'Even a boy such as yourself can appreciate how your fellow prisoners will feel about you should you be the cause of their distress.' He leant close to Chad's face. 'You will be most unpopular. We are placing you into the section with the other modified humans. You may notice you can reach the human prisoners through the bars.'

So this is how it is, I thought. *There are mods and there are humans.*

Suddenly I'm not human anymore. I'm a mod. A different life form.

'I advise you not to eat the humans,' the guard said. 'Many of them are diseased.'

The comment was so ridiculous I expected the guard to suddenly burst into laughter. To my surprise his face only grew more serious.

'Food will arrive tomorrow morning,' he said. 'I advise you to remain alert. Twenty percent of new inmates do not survive their first night.'

Lee turned his back and the guards relocked

the gate. We watched them as they mounted the stairs. The door above opened and they exited through it. The only sound was that of a fire burning somewhere in the open chamber.

Chad and I glanced at each other. We had to find Zachary Stead, but we could not simply go around asking for him. We had to make his acquaintance and gradually gain his trust. This would be a slow process, but we had to speed it up as much as possible.

I looked into the shadows all around us. There were men in the shadows. Most of them looked filthy and unwell although a few of them were larger and fitter. A long, drawn out cry came from the human section. It was cut off mid breath. From somewhere in the mod section—a dark corner to our right—we heard a laugh.

The person laughed for about a minute before the sound developed into a wail and finally the sound became weeping.

'Not the happiest of places,' Chad commented.

'Not really,' I agreed.

Slowly I realized three men were making their way from one of the dark recesses. The middle of the three was a small, scrawny looking man with long, thin hair and a small stubble beard. It was impossible to tell his age. His companions were larger than us, maybe aged in their thirties. The closer they drew the more I realized they were built like wrestlers. It crossed my mind that maybe the story of cannibalism wasn't so crazy after all.

'I'm Becker,' the man in the middle said. 'We like new blood in this place. New people bring in new things. Things we can use.'

'Like what?' I asked.

He looked down at our feet. 'Shoes are good,' he said. 'I like shoes.'

'You should get out and buy some,' Chad said.

We were ready for anything. Despite the size of this guy's friends, Chad had his powers and—hopefully—I had mine.

'I don't think so,' Becker said. 'Anyway, you

won't be needing shoes.'

'And why is that?' I asked.

'Why would someone with no feet need shoes?' he asked.

Suddenly I realized I was looking up at Becker from the ground. What was going on? Then I looked back to my legs and a scream caught in my throat. Both Chad and I were on the dirty ground. Our legs were gone. Just below our pelvises, our legs had been removed and the wounds neatly cauterized and expertly treated. All we had left, where our legs used to be, were stumps.

I looked up at Becker in horror. He had both our pairs of shoes in his hands.

'Thanks boys,' he said. 'Welcome to Yodak.'

Chapter Twenty

Ethan Craddock was as good as his word. When Brodie and Ebony turned up to meet the FBI agent, he appeared from behind a clump of trees and drew them to one side away from the rubbish area.

He spent the next twenty minutes explaining to them about the Doomsday virus and Jeremiah Stead's intention to release the weapon into the atmosphere. By the time he finished speaking, both girls were stunned into silence.

Finally Brodie said, 'But surely he's going to kill everyone inside the compound as well. After the virus spreads—'

'The virus has a very short life,' Ethan said. 'It dies quite quickly. Once it wipes the planet bare it will extinguish itself. Jeremiah and his people will leave the compound and repopulate the earth.'

Brodie felt sick. 'We have to stop him.'

'We have to stop Ferdy,' Ebony said. 'The virus is safe as long as the canister remains closed. If Ferdy opens it—'

'How likely is that?' Ethan asked. 'I've been told you teenagers have some special sorts of powers.'

Brodie turned to Ebony. 'You know Ferdy better than me. What do you think?'

'He's smart,' Ebony said thoughtfully. 'Very smart. And not just in a memory retention type of way. I found one of those Rubik's Cubes at a market and gave it to Ferdy to solve.'

'Anyone can solve those,' Ethan said. 'The instructions are on the net.'

'He had never seen one before,' Ebony said. 'And he did it without looking at the net. It took him about a minute.'

One minute, Brodie thought. *If he could do that in one minute then in a few hours or days...*

'We need to stop your friend,' Ethan said. 'But I need to get out of here.'

'Why haven't you left already?' Brodie asked, looking around. 'It looks like the security is pretty lax.'

'It looks that way,' Ethan said. 'But there are

cameras in all the trees. They monitor all the foot traffic for miles around. If I tried to leave here without a good reason they would kill me.'

'Just for trying to leave?' Ebony asked in amazement.

He shook his head in dismay. 'I've seen people killed for not cleaning their weapons properly. I've seen them killed for playing inappropriate music inside the compound. Stead rules with an iron fist. He allows no dissent. These people are completely brainwashed. They see him as some kind of God.'

'That's terrible,' Ebony said. 'Does the FBI know where you are?'

'No. I joined the Sanctuary group in Ohio and was brought here before I could get a message out.'

'I wish we had phones,' Brodie said. 'It would be so easy to simply ring someone.'

'There are no phones,' Ethan said. 'Likewise, there is no news from outside allowed into the complex.' He hesitated. 'I assume, for example, that Canada has not been invaded by the UN?'

'Huh?' Brodie said.

'I thought as much,' Ethan said sadly. 'Jeremiah gave a lecture the other day telling everyone the UN had invaded Canada. Toronto and other major cities had been bombed with nuclear devices.'

'That's the most ridiculous thing I've ever heard,' Brodie said.

'You'll hear some pretty ridiculous things here,' Ethan said. 'Whatever you do, don't contradict Jeremiah.'

Ebony looked annoyed. 'He doesn't like healthy debate?'

'Freedom of speech ends at the front gate,' Ethan said. 'A newcomer disagreed with Jeremiah about three months ago during one of the meals. The next day when we went to eat breakfast we found the new guy hanging upside-down from one of the trees with his throat cut.'

'That's terrible!' Brodie said.

'As we ate our meal we had to listen to Jeremiah lecturing to us about the importance of truth and justice while this poor person's body waved in the wind.' He shook his head. 'It was sickening.'

Ethan looked at his watch. 'I need to get back otherwise I'll be missed.'

'What do we do now?' Brodie asked.

'You need to find your friend and get yourselves out of here,' Ethan said. 'Once you're out of here contact the authorities and get this place closed down.'

Ethan suggested he return to the compound first and the girls start back a few minutes later. It would appear suspicious for them to arrive together. After Ethan left, Ebony turned to Brodie.

'We need to find where they're keeping Ferdy,' she said.

'He has to be our number one priority,' Brodie agreed.

They walked back to the compound, entered the building and made their way back down to the main hall. There were people in small groups singing songs. The songs seemed to be about how the New World Order would be defeated by The Chosen Few. Others were sitting around in groups and reading from some of the survival literature.

Jason sighted them from the other side of the room. He gave Brodie a friendly wave and crossed over.

'May I speak to you?' he asked Brodie. 'In private?'

Brodie looked at Ebony. The other girl nodded.

'I'll check on Dan,' Ebony said. 'I'll see if he's feeling better.'

After she left, Jason indicated a small open room to the side of the main chamber. They sat on two wooden chairs. Brodie wondered what this was about. She hoped their meeting with Ethan had not aroused suspicion.

'We need to speak about our future,' Jason said.

'What future is that?' Brodie asked.

'The End Times are coming very soon,' Jason said. 'I know you have powers. You are not like normal people.'

'I'm a little faster than most people,' Brodie

said noncommittally. 'If that's what you mean.'

'I'm trying to say that doesn't make any difference to me. My father has said I must take a wife who is a daughter of Isis.'

'Really?' Brodie said.

I have no idea what you're talking about, she thought.

'I have spoken to my father and he supports my choice,' Jason said. 'I will be married and you are to become my wife.'

Chapter Twenty-One

My legs were gone. I wanted to scream. In fact I think a sound actually escaped my lips as I stared in horror at the place where my legs used to be. Looking over at Chad I saw he was similarly horrified.

A laugh came from the shadows. 'Everyone gets caught first time around,' the voice said. 'It's an illusion.'

It took a few moments for the words to sink in. I looked into the shadows and saw a man sitting back against the wall shaking his head in amusement.

'Wh-what?' I gasped. 'What are you saying?'

'It's an illusion,' the man repeated. 'That's Becker's modification. Just shake your head and it'll clear.'

I looked down at my legs. For the first time I noticed I was wearing shorts. How could I be wearing shorts? Even if Becker had some magical ability to sever my legs, there was no way he could make new clothing appear from nowhere.

My legs began to reappear. Like a ghostly image appearing on a film they came back into view. At the same time I gave a cry of amazement—and relief. My legs were not gone. They were still attached to my body. I grabbed them with joy.

Chad was still fixated by the hallucination. I scrambled over to him.

'Listen to me,' I said. 'It's just an illusion. It's all in your mind.'

'What? No, my legs—'

I shook him. 'It's not real. Look! Your legs are still there!'

Chad looked down and slowly the terror slid from his face replaced by relief. He ran his hands up and down his legs. Slowly he stood up, looking at them in amazement.

'You're right,' he said. 'Thank God. Thank—' His face twisted into an expression of fury. 'I'm going to kill that guy.'

'Later,' the voice called from the shadows. 'He's the least of your worries down here.'

I grabbed Chad's arm and slowly led him into

the alcove. Two men were in there. One of them was asleep. The one who was awake was sitting back on a bench. He was dressed in little more than rags.

'Thanks for the advice,' I said.

'Advice is free,' he said. 'Do you want some more?'

'Sure.'

'Snitches get stitches,' he said.

'Which means?'

'We don't speak to the guards,' he said. 'We tell them nothing. If you snitch on an inmate your life won't be worth living.'

I nodded. 'What's your name?'

'They call me Drink,' he said.

'Drink?' Chad said. 'That's a pretty strange name.'

The man grinned. In the next instant he seemed to turn translucent then before Chad or I could say anything he turned completely to water. He splashed onto the floor into a puddle. While we stared open mouthed at him, he just as quickly reformed into a human being.

'Still think it's a strange name?' Drink asked.

'How do you do that?' I asked.

'I'm a mod,' he said. 'You are too otherwise you wouldn't be in here.'

I nodded. I wasn't about to reveal my powers, but Chad had no such qualms. He held his hands out. In one hand he produced a ball of fire. In the other he held a ball of snow.

'An elemental. That's good. That'll help you survive in here.' He looked at me. 'What are you?'

'I've got some abilities,' I said. 'I might show you later.'

He nodded. 'Keeping it close to home. Clever.'

'How did you become a mod?' Chad asked.

'I was in an Israeli jail,' he said. 'They made me an offer. I could be part of an experiment or I could spend the rest of my life in jail. I decided to be a guinea pig.' He continued. 'I didn't know the Americans were doing modifications. I thought they were following the UN ruling.'

'What ruling?' I asked.

'Don't you boys know anything?' he asked. 'Sit down and I'll tell you the facts of life.'

We sat down on the bench next to him.

'You know mods have been around for centuries,' he said.

'You mean, like vampires?' I said.

'Vampires and all the others,' Drink said. 'They were the natural mods. As soon as the enlightenment began, people started manipulating the human creature to improve upon it. You've heard of Frankenstein, of course.'

'Yeah, but you don't mean—'

'It's a fictional story,' Drink said. 'But it's based on fact. Governments had been experimenting in secret for years trying to create soldiers that would give them an advantage in combat. After WW2, upon the formation of the UN, it was decided to ban all human modifications.'

'So no more modifications were allowed,' Chad said.

'They weren't allowed,' Drink explained. 'But they still happened. Oh, not all countries and not all the time. And it's a dangerous process. Most mods die within days of the process. A lot don't last a year. But the ones that do last…'

He pointed to himself.

'So what are you doing here?' I asked.

'All mods discovered on foreign territory are supposed to be in jail,' he said. 'You know that? Right?'

'Uh, no,' I said.

'Hell,' he shook his head. 'You boys really are green. Didn't you get told anything?'

'Not really.'

'I was spying for the Israelis,' Drink explained. 'I got caught. How did you boys end up in this predicament?'

'A prisoner exchange,' I said.

Drink nodded. 'Sounds fair enough. Most governments treat their mods like commodities to be traded or killed. A lot of governments kill foreign mods immediately.'

Holy hell, I thought.

'Why are you still here?' I asked. 'With your

ability to change to water—'

'A similar deal that put you boys in here is going to get me out,' he said. 'My country has a North Korean mod in custody. In a few weeks they'll do the exchange and I'll be out of here.'

A gong rang; a long reverberating bell that chimed throughout the whole jail.

'They're putting the lights out soon boys,' Drink said.

As soon as he said the words, the whole jail went dark. The only light to be seen was from a few random fires still burning.

'When morning comes there'll be a fight for food,' Drink explained. 'It's every man for himself.'

'Do you mean—' I started.

'No offense,' Drink said. 'I like you boys, but I haven't eaten for two days. I'm going to fight you and whoever else I have to so I can survive.'

For a long time the only sound was the crackling of fire.

'May the best man win,' Drink said.

Chapter Twenty-Two

'Wife?' Brodie wasn't sure she had heard Jason correctly. 'Did you just say—'

'You are to become my wife,' Jason confirmed. He looked quite earnest. Almost as if he was discussing the weather. 'It has been decided. All that needs to be determined now is when the marriage will happen.'

'I'll tell you when,' Brodie said. 'Never.'

She felt like she was going crazy. Jason seemed like a pleasant enough guy. He even came across as being reasonably intelligent. How could he think it would be okay to be in an arranged marriage?

He looked confused. 'What do you mean?'

Brodie remembered what Ethan had said about directly challenging the beliefs of the Sanctuary residents. Despite the apparent freedom they had been granted, their lives still lay on a knife edge. The worst thing she could do would be to cause a fight— especially with the Jeremiah's son.

She said as gently as possible, 'You're a nice

guy, Jason. A very nice guy. But I barely know you.'

'You don't need to know me,' he said.

'Yes I do. When I get married it has to be for love.'

Jason looked at her bemused. 'You don't understand, do you?'

'Understand what?'

'My father has decided we are to be together,' he said. 'He has been deliberating ever since you arrived. He knew you were special. That's why he took you from the outside world.'

'Jason,' she said. 'I really can't marry you.'

'Why?'

Why? This could go on all day. Why couldn't you marry a person you've known for twenty-four hours? If you have to ask such a question…

'Because it's the wrong thing to do,' she said. 'I'm already in love with someone else.'

Jason looked shocked. 'I'm very sorry to hear that.'

'You're sorry…'

'I'm sorry because everyone outside the

compound will be dead in a week,' Jason said. 'The cleansing is coming. The time for the old era to pass is upon us. A new world, a better world is coming.' He reached out and took her hand. 'I'm sorry for you.'

Brodie had an overwhelming feeling that she wanted to punch him in the face, but took great care to keep her emotions in check. She gently released her hand and gave him a small smile, not wanting to completely ostracize him. She decided to try to talk some sense into the boy. 'Can you explain to me why it's all right to kill billions of people? I mean, it seems a little dramatic, don't you think?'

'The UN has given us no choice,' Jason said patiently. 'They have gradually taken over more and more countries over this last year. China and Canada have fallen in the last few months.'

'You're saying all those countries have been invaded by the United Nations?' Brodie said.

'Yes, of course.'

'What if I were to say to you that nothing has changed in those countries.'

'What do you mean?'

'I'm saying those countries are still operating as they always have.'

'I don't understand what you mean,' Jason looked confused. 'My father has been giving us weekly reports on the invasions.'

'Invasions?' This was just too ridiculous for words. 'Let me ask you this, Jason.'

'Okay.'

'The peacekeeping arm of the UN is made up of troops from dozens of different countries. Still, it's a big planet and it barely has enough troops for its normal peacekeeping missions.' She let this information set in. 'How could it possibly invade a country like Canada? Or China for that matter.'

'I'm sure they were taken by surprise.'

'Taken by—' This kid was cuckoo. 'Jason, it must have been one hell of a surprise. And China has nuclear weapons. It has one of the largest armies on Earth. How could it be taken by surprise?'

Jason shook his head. 'I don't know the details—'

'There are no details to know,' Brodie said. 'Your father is lying to you.'

'You mustn't say such things.' Jason's face turned white with anger. 'My father was chosen by God! Are you so stupid you can't see that?'

This was getting waaay out of hand. Jason was getting so loud that people were starting to stare.

'I don't want to offend your father,' Brodie said. 'I know you must love him very much.'

'I do!' Jason snapped. 'We all do.'

He looked down in despair. For almost an entire minute he did not speak. He simply stared down at the floor. Brodie wondered if he might be praying. Finally he looked up at her. At least now the color had returned to his cheeks.

'I'm sorry I lost my temper,' he said.

Brodie nodded.

'I know you're ignorant,' Jason said. 'Like all the others out there. You need to be educated.'

You're the one who needs education, Brodie thought.

'What sort of education are you thinking of?'

Brodie asked.

'We have books, videos—'

'It might help if I could see the whole compound,' Brodie said, pretending to look around. She realized she could pretend to show a romantic interest in Jason, but that might be taking things too far. 'I've hardly seen any of it.'

'I can give you a tour,' Jason said.

His good humor seemed to have recovered.

'Can we make a time?' Brodie asked.

'How about after lunch?'

'That would be fine.' Brodie stood. 'I better go and check on my friend Dan. I want to make certain he's feeling better.'

Jason nodded and gave her a wave as she left.

Brodie gave a long sigh as soon as she was out of sight. That didn't go very well. Not well at all. If Jason was any indication of the way people thought here, then changing their minds would be almost impossible.

When she arrived back at their room on one of the lower levels she found Ebony sitting in the chamber alone.

'Where's Dan?' Brodie asked.

'Gone.'

'Where?'

'I have no idea. The room was empty when I arrived.'

Brodie left and found Susan.

'That's right,' Susan confirmed. 'He has been moved to another room.'

'Where is he?'

'I don't know. You'll have to ask Jeremiah or Jason.'

Brodie went storming through the complex looking for them. By the time she found Jeremiah she had reminded herself how important it was to remain calm. She and Ebony had the run of the complex so far. It would be a mistake to jeopardize all that by flying off the handle.

The compound leader and Donna were in deep discussion as she approached.

'Jeremiah!' she called.

'Ah,' he said. 'It's one of our newest

members.'

'Where is Dan? It looks like he's been moved.'

'He has,' Jeremiah confirmed. 'Now that we are in the final days it is important to plan for the future.'

Which meant...?

'He is now sharing a dormitory with some of our members who are closer in age,' Jeremiah said. 'It's more appropriate.'

'Can I see him?'

'That wouldn't be a good idea.'

A hundred responses went through Brodie's head. She felt like punching the man in the head and turning every room upside down until she found Dan. But where would that get them? They still had to find Ferdy and he could be anywhere. She had to do the hardest thing now and that was to remain silent. Try to gain their trust. Wait for the right moment to arrive.

'All right,' Brodie said.

'Jason tells me he's showing you around the compound after lunch.'

'Yes he is.'

Brodie expected him to forbid the tour.

'Have a nice time,' Jeremiah said.

Brodie turned to leave.

'Just one thing,' Jeremiah continued.

'Yes?'

'Welcome to the family.'

Chapter Twenty-Three

The serving of breakfast bore more resemblance to feeding time at a farm than a presentation of food for inmates in a jail. Although I doubted I would sleep at all, I found myself dead to the world until the lights flickered on at some ungodly hour. It was impossible to determine the time and we had relinquished our watches before embarking on the mission.

Chad made some inarticulate sounds as he struggled into wakefulness. Drink was off the bench immediately and warily crouched near the entrance to the chamber peering out into the main area.

I stood near him.

'What are you waiting for?' I asked.

He looked like he didn't want to answer me. Finally he said, 'You see those enclosures in the ceiling?'

I did. They were at regular intervals about ten feet apart.

'Food drops out of them,' Drink said.

I could see the immediate problem. 'How do you know which one?'

'You don't know. The guards place bets on who isn't going to make it and then draw lots on where to drop the food. If it lands near us we're lucky. If it doesn't…'

He looked over to the darkened alcoves on the opposite side of the enclosure.

'Are they dangerous?' I asked.

'Everyone's dangerous,' he answered. 'If you're hungry enough.'

A sound came from behind us.

'What's up, people?' Chad asked.

I grabbed his arm. 'Wake up, you idiot. Food's on its way.'

'Food? Great, I'll start with bacon and eggs, then some pancakes—'

Three slots opened up in the ceiling. They were all close to the middle of the room. A pile of food fell through. It looked more like a heap of garbage. No sooner had it hit the floor than Drink started toward it. At the same time a creature that looked like a cross between a tiger and a lizard leapt out of one of the alcoves.

'What the—' Chad started.

'We need to get some of this,' I told him.

'Are you mad?'

I activated my air powers, using it to drag some of the refuse toward us. Drink tried fighting with the cat man over a loaf of bread. Mods appeared from everywhere. Fist fights started. A man about three times the width of a normal person started punching into a very tall, thin man who fired electricity from his hands. Another guy seemed to be fighting with thin air; then I realized I could faintly see a mist. Obviously he could transform himself into a porous gas.

Becker tried using his powers to mesmerize another one of the inmates—a well built, black man with extra arms—but the man simply punched him in the face, smashing him to the ground.

I had the loaf of bread in my hands by the time Chad started out of the cell. For a second I thought he was going for more food. Then I realized he was going to help Drink. The water man was fighting a losing battle. His ability to change into water was also his weakness. He could not grasp any of the food without reverting back to human. Every time he tried, the cat man took another swipe at him.

Finally Drink's head hit the ground. Momentarily dazed, the cat man pulled a clawed hand back to deliver the fatal blow.

Bam! Bam! Bam!

Three icy rocks hit the creature in the head and it went flying. Chad followed up with a blast of fire that singed its hairs. It leapt out of the way. I wondered if I should try for more food, but Drink used the opportunity to rouse himself and grab some pieces of fruit. He staggered back to the enclosure.

'This is easy,' Chad said, turning to me. 'Once I've had my bacon—'

A blast of energy struck Chad across the back of the head. He went flying. It was like a rock, but it was a shade of clear red light and dissipated as soon as it struck Chad. Another blast flew at him, but this time I threw up a shield and blocked it. Keeping my shield in position, I dropped the loaf of bread and grabbed Chad. I dragged him back to our enclosure.

By now the fighting had come to an end. All the food was gone. Anyone that could move was back in their alcove. Two people were motionless. One of them was Becker. The other was a thin man who, out of the corner of my eye, I had seen climbing the walls like a spider. It had not helped him.

Someone had knocked him unconscious and he lay unmoving.

By now Chad was regaining consciousness.

'What hit me?' he groaned.

'An energy blast,' I said. 'Someone out there packs quite a punch.'

'I'll say,' he groaned. 'Did we get some food?'

I looked around for my loaf of bread, but it was gone. I looked up at Drink, but he was sitting back on the bench gnawing on a piece of fruit.

'Where did our bread go?' I asked.

He shrugged, but his eyes subtly shifted to his left. The man on the bench, the man who had not moved since we had arrived, was sitting on the bench gnawing on the loaf.

'That's our bread!' I yelled.

He looked at me impassively.

'So?' he said.

'So I want it back.'

The man simply stared and said nothing. He just continued to eat the bread.

Chad had recovered by now and glared at the quiet man on the bench.

'Didn't you hear my friend?' he said. 'We want our bread back.'

'Maybe you should come and take it,' he suggested.

I didn't like the way he said that. Before I could say anything, Chad raised a hand and blasted ice balls toward him. The man raised his hand and the balls flew back and slammed Chad in the face. They hit him so hard this time his head flew back and he hit the ground unconscious.

'Didn't they teach you kids at school?' the man asked mildly. 'Every action has an equal and opposite reaction.' He took another bite of the bread. 'By the way, they call me Recoil.'

Chapter Twenty-Four

Dan had been sitting in the room alone for about an hour when a knock sounded at the door.

'Come in,' he said.

A young girl appeared. She looked to be about his age. Fourteen or fifteen. She had a friendly, good natured face, brown hair and eyes and dimples in her cheeks. She gave Dan a pleasant smile.

'I'm Sally,' she said. 'How are you feeling?'

'Okay, I guess.'

Actually okay was a rather inaccurate description of how he felt. He didn't remember very much about the last few days. He remembered the fire. Their house had been alight. He remembered the vampires. One of them—a woman—had come into his room and before he had a chance to even climb out of bed, she had fired a dart gun at him.

Within seconds he had passed out.

After that everything was confusion. He could remember waking up in a truck, but everything was moving around him. He could see Brodie's and then

Ebony's face coming into view, but could not recall anything they were saying to him. He recalled wanting to vomit and his head spinning so badly the world seemed to be on an axis.

Then night seemed to have fallen, a deep endless night from which he had only just awoken.

Now he found himself looking at a pretty face with a disarming smile.

Still, he had to be careful.

'Are you a vampire?' he asked. 'I have powers if you are.'

The girl laughed. 'That's silly. No, I'm just a girl. Someone wants to see you.'

'Who?'

'Jeremiah. He's the leader of the Sanctuary compound.'

'Is that where I am? The Sanctuary compound?'

She nodded.

'Where are my friends?' Dan asked.

'Jeremiah will answer all your questions,' Sally said. 'He's a very wise man.' She left the room.

A moment later she stuck her head back in. 'Hey silly, are you coming?'

It looks like I am, Dan thought.

He followed the girl into the passageway and found himself in an underground building. It reminded him a lot of The Agency. A man and woman passed him in the hallway. They gave him a friendly smile and said hello. Dan tried to appear confident, but beneath the surface he felt quite nervous.

'You didn't tell me your name,' Sally said.

'My name is Dan.'

'Dan? As in Dan the Man?' Sally said. 'That's a cool name.'

'Thanks.'

'I was named after Sally Fields. The actress.'

'I don't know her.'

'She was pretty famous.'

Dan had pretty much made up his mind that he wasn't in the vampire's lair. He carefully felt around his neck and found it free of bite marks. That was a good start. He had mentioned his powers to the girl.

Maybe he shouldn't have done that, but this girl—Sally—didn't seem nervous or confused.

At least he had his powers. Of course, he appeared to be deep inside some enormous underground structure. He didn't relish the idea of trying to fight his way out of here. Sally pushed a door open and led him into a large meeting room containing an oval table surrounded by chairs. A man sat at one of the chairs reading a book. Dan could not make out the words on the cover.

'Ah, welcome,' the man said. 'I'm glad you're doing better now.'

'H-hello,' Dan said. He didn't want to sound nervous, so he lowered his voice to sound older.

'I understand your name is Dan,' the man said.

'Yes. It is.'

'My name is Jeremiah Stead,' the man said, placing the book down. 'Sally, would you be so kind as to sit with Dan while I explain how he ended up in this crazy situation?'

Dan sat down as Sally took the chair next to

him. He was certain this was the man behind his kidnapping. Looking around, he tried to look for objects made from metal. The chairs seemed to have a metal base. If he had to escape he could probably use them as a weapon.

'Where are my friends?' Dan asked.

'They're close by,' Jeremiah said. 'First of all, I want to apologize for bringing you here under these circumstances. These are desperate times and I had to resort to desperate measures.'

'Okay,' Dan said, although he had no idea to what he was agreeing.

'I see you've already made one friend,' Jeremiah said. 'Sally is a lovely girl. She had already told me how handsome you were.'

Sally gave an embarrassed laugh. Dan looked at her and was pleasantly surprised to see her blushing.

'Your friends—Ferdy in particular—are helping me in a project I'm working on.'

'What kind of project?' Dan asked suspiciously.

'I have a particular code I'm trying to decipher,' Jeremiah said. 'I believe your friend Ferdy can help me.'

Dan decided he didn't believe a word of what this man was saying. There were ways to go about asking for help. They did not include using vampires to kidnap a bunch of kids from their home and locking them in an underground bunker.

'I understand you're an orphan, Dan,' Jeremiah suddenly changed tact.

'Uh, yes.' Dan felt a bit self conscious. He had barely spoken to the others about being an orphan, but almost every night he thought about his parents. Axel had mentioned dreams he had about a wheat field and a farm, but for Dan there had been no similar memories. Like the others, he could remember his life after being experimented on by The Agency. Everything before that was a blank.

Thinking about his parents always made him feel a bit empty.

'I'm an orphan too,' Jeremiah said. 'My parents passed away when I was very young. There's nothing like that terrible feeling of being ultimately alone.'

Jeremiah seemed to be speaking almost to Dan's heart. He could feel a choking sensation in his throat.

The man gave his shoulder a squeeze. 'We want to treat you like a member of our family, Dan.'

'When can I see my friends?' Dan asked.

'Soon,' Jeremiah promised. 'Very soon. In the meantime I'd like you to get to know some of the people here at Sanctuary. Sally?'

'Yes, Jeremiah?'

'I want you to take Dan to the shared accommodation room, but before I do I have to ask him two questions.'

'Yes sir?' Dan said.

'One. Do you like lots of fun?' Jeremiah asked.

'Uh, yes.'

The man gave him a friendly smile. 'I'm afraid it's fun unlimited in the dorm with the kids. Even I go down there when I'm feeling a bit down.'

'Okay.'

'And question two.' Jeremiah took a deep breath. 'I need an honest answer to this, Dan.'

'Sir?'

'Do you like being called Dan the Man?'

Dan couldn't help but smile. 'Yes sir. I do.'

Jeremiah held out his hand and shook Dan's hand. 'I christen you Dan the Man. I will make certain everyone calls you that from now on.'

'Okay.' Dan found himself feeling quite good. Almost euphoric. This Jeremiah character was really a good guy.

'And just one thing, my boy,' Jeremiah said just before Dan passed through the door.

'Yes, sir?'

'Don't forget who your friends are.'

'I won't,' Dan promised.

After Dan left the room, Jeremiah sat back in his chair. He formed a steeple with his fingers.

Everything was going according to plan. Exactly as he wanted it.

He began to laugh.

Chapter Twenty-Five

We had survived our first day, but only by the skin of our teeth.

Chad was bruised and battered and resentful about Recoil and his abilities. We had sat quietly together and I had done my best to keep him calm. His face and head were a mess. He had tried to talk me into joining him in an assault on Recoil, but I thought it a bad idea.

'Why?' he hissed, quietly furious.

Recoil had gone back to his position on the bench, his back turned to us, apparently asleep.

'Because we're not ready,' I told him. 'And we're not here to get into fights with inmates. We're here to find Zachary Stead.'

'We'll starve before that happens,' Chad protested. 'We need to survive in the meantime.'

I couldn't argue too much with what he was saying. I was growing hungry. We had not eaten all day. The next food would arrive tomorrow morning and we would be weaker than today.

'There must be a way around this,' I said. 'Why do we have to fight like animals?'

'You and Ghandi would get along great.'

This made me think. 'You might have something there.'

'You're thinking about ringing up Mahatma Ghandi and starting a peaceful protest?' Chad asked. Despite his injuries he was still sarcastic. If ever we couldn't tell if Chad were dead or alive we would simply check his sarcasm; if it was intact, he was alive.

'It's a little too late for Ghandi—' I began.

'You think?'

'—but not for attempting a peaceful solution.'

I walked out into the open area of the compound.

'Can I have everyone's attention, please?' I called. Without waiting for a response, I continued. 'My friend and I are only new here, but we want to suggest a plan.'

I looked over to our alcove. Drink was sitting up and watching in curiosity. Even Recoil had rolled over and was watching the proceedings. From somewhere on the other side of the compound I heard a laugh. A long, laugh without the slightest trace of humor.

'There's obviously not enough food to go around,' I said. 'But we need to share the food we have. Together we can get through this. The guards want us to fight each other, but our enemy is—'

Something flew at me. A red ball of light that would have hit me, but for Chad's quick action. He threw up an ice barrier that rebounded the shot away.

'That's what we don't need,' I said. 'You're just playing into the guard's hands—'

This time the cat man leapt from the darkness, but this time I was prepared for him. I threw a force field of compressed air at him and knocked him to the ground. At the same time the other mod who was able to fire the laser beams came out of the darkness and fired a long, sustained blast at me.

I was able to keep him at bay, but already the cat man was rising to his feet. He took a running jump straight toward me—

—and straight into a block of ice.

Chad was fast. Gotta give him that.

Another mod sprang from the shadows. This one I had not seen before. He moved incredibly quickly—he was even faster than Brodie. He raced straight toward Chad. Before I could even try to warn him, the stranger had landed a punch in the middle of Chad's face. The cat man seized the initiative and hurled himself at Chad.

This situation was completely out of control. I tried to extend my shield, but it was too late. The three of them started rolling about on the ground. Suddenly a burst of heat leapt from Chad straight into the cat man. The mod let out an inhuman scream and began to roll about on the ground on fire.

Firing a burst of hurricane wind at the speedster, I threw him toward a wall and he lay still.

Recoil sauntered to the door of the alcove. 'Having fun, boys?'

How I longed to wipe that smirk off his face, but at that moment another sustained burst of power was directed toward me. Much to my surprise Recoil ran forward into the beam. The burst was reflected back to my assailant and I heard a scream emanate from the darkness.

The beam stopped. The cat man struggled to his feet and retreated back into the darkness as did the speedster.

So much for diplomacy. My efforts had gained us exactly—nothing. Chad picked himself up from the ground and staggered over to me. He had a set of large cuts across his shoulder where the cat man had torn his skin. Recoil eyed the wounds.

'That's a serious wound you've got there,' he said. 'It's a shame you can't get that seen to.'

'It's okay,' Chad shrugged.

'It's not,' Recoil said. 'Stalker's scratches infect whoever he cuts. You'll probably die.'

Oh great, I thought. *Things just get better and better in this place.*

'So is there a cure?' I asked.

'Sure,' Recoil replied. 'It's called death.'

'There is a cure,' a voice said from behind us.

We turned around. A man on the human side

of the metal cage was walking from the shadows toward the bars. So far we had barely glimpsed anyone on that side. It seemed the humans suffered in silence, but made a point of staying out of the light. After seeing one or more of their number used as food it was probably the wisest course of action.

'A plant grows on the outside of the jail,' the man explained. 'A purple flower. One of the guards was injured by cat man and he was saved through applying the flower to his wound.'

'So how do we get the flower?' I asked.

Recoil laughed. 'Tell the guards you need some flowers for your girlfriend.'

The stranger continued to linger at the bars as Recoil returned to the darkened alcove.

'I feel fine,' Chad said. 'I don't know what all the worry is about.'

'You feel fine now,' the man said. 'You won't later.'

I sidled up to the bars. 'My name is Axel.'

'My name is Zachary,' the man introduced himself.

I felt like jumping for joy. This was Zachary—the man we had come here to find! I managed to hide my excitement while I introduced Chad.

'By morning you will be quite unwell,' Zachary said to Chad. 'Your illness will become progressively worse. By tomorrow night you will barely be able to walk. The morning after…'

'What about the morning after?' Chad asked.

'It is unlikely you will last that long,' Zachary said. 'Best to enjoy your next few hours. They will be your last.'

Chapter Twenty-Six

Jeremiah was thinking about evolution.

He was a big believer in evolution. He believed in Darwin's ideas about a creature fitting an environment as neatly as a piece in a jigsaw puzzle. The creatures that survived in an environment deserved to survive. There was a certain justice to it; a balance that kept the world from spiraling out of control.

Humans, of course, had upset that balance and now he was about to redress it.

It had all started with the formation of the United Nations. For centuries the greatest fear for people was that the world would one day fall under the crushing oppression of a single world government. With the creation of the United Nations, this terrible plan was finally set in motion. As the world hovered on the brink of destruction, a savior had to arise. Someone had to save the human race from itself.

That someone was Jeremiah Stead.

God himself had spoken to him. God had instructed him that the old way had to fall and a new, everlasting order would reign on Earth. Jeremiah had been planning his own New World Order for almost twenty years.

Finally, after all these days of planning, his time had come.

A knock sounded at the door of the meeting room.

His son.

'Jason,' Jeremiah said. 'What is it?'

'A man has arrived,' Jason said. 'He has asked to see you.'

'What is his name?'

'A general,' Jason said. 'A man named Wolff.'

Jeremiah nodded. He had been expecting Mr. Wolff for some time.

'Show him in.'

Jason disappeared and a moment later returned with Solomon Wolff. The man was an imposing figure. He had been described to Jeremiah by Mercer Todd as someone who could get the job done. Mercer Todd had been correct. Wolff had delivered the boy known as Ferdy—and his friends—to the Sanctuary Compound exactly as promised.

Unfortunately, not everything had gone completely according to plan.

'General,' he greeted him. 'Welcome back to Sanctuary.'

'Jeremiah.' Wolff shook hands with him. 'I trust all has been going well.'

Both men sat.

'Like all things in life,' Jeremiah said. 'There have been ups and downs.'

'Really.' Wolff managed to look both interested and a little bored at the same time. 'I trust that has not affected our arrangement.'

'Your operatives delivered the boy to me. And his friends. They will fit quite well with our plans,' Jeremiah said. 'I thank you for that.'

Wolff nodded.

'But there has been a problem with the boy,' Jeremiah continued.

'Really.'

'I needed him to help with the breaking of a cipher. A code.'

'I know what a cipher is.'

'And his abnormality has stood in the way.'

'That is not my problem.' Wolff spoke directly. 'My role was to bring him and the others to you. That task was completed. Now there is the small matter of money.' He paused. 'Or a rather large matter. One hundred million dollars.'

'Your money will come.'

'So will Christmas,' Wolff said.

Not this year, Jeremiah thought.

He decided it best not to contradict his guest.

'My ability to pay is dependent on having the boy break the code,' Jeremiah said. 'When the code is broken you will receive payment.'

It was a lie, of course. As far as Jeremiah was concerned, Wolff would never receive his payment. His goal was to delay him for the next few days until the Barricade cipher was broken. Once that happened, well, a whole new world would exist. A world without money. A world without bills. A world without Wolff.

All he needed was a few more days.

'That was not our agreement,' Wolff said. 'Payment was to arrive within hours of the boy being handed over.'

Wolff was annoyed with himself. He had made an amateur's mistake. He had not received payment prior to completing the exercise. Promises were easily made, but not so easily kept. Everyone was very obliging until money was due to be delivered, but once the bill became due they often changed tune. Wolff knew he should have collected his money ahead of time or at the point of delivery.

This is an amateur's mistake, Wolff thought. *I've been around for too long to make mistakes like this.*

Looking at Jeremiah he knew the man was tall and strong and in good shape for his age. In many fights he could probably hold his own. Possibly even win.

But he could not beat Wolff.

At this very moment General Wolff could think of no less than eighteen different ways to kill Jeremiah Stead. He knew another twenty methods where Jeremiah could be disabled and never walk again. Another handful of techniques would remove his sight, hearing or tongue.

Possibly the most interesting skill at Wolff's disposal was the ability to paralyze a person, leaving them aware and reasoning, but unable to make a sound or move a muscle. The unfortunate victim would spend the rest of their life in a hospital bed without hope of recovery.

Still, all was not lost.

Wolff had not survived this long by killing his customers. He recalled something one of his early mentors had said to him.

'There are always many roads to the sea.'

'This cipher must be quite a unique device,' Wolff said conversationally.

'It is very unique. Once opened it will release a deadly weapon that will change the world. Forever.'

Wolff felt a shudder of concern. In his

business people were always boasting about new and efficient killing machines. In this case, however, he didn't like the use of the word release.

Release had its own rather unique meaning and Wolff had heard a rumor that a virus had been stolen. An Armageddon virus. Such a thing was not to be trifled with.

While killing innocents did not concern him, killing the population of the planet—including himself—was bad for business no matter how it was viewed.

'I wish I had known your intentions,' Wolff said. 'I know someone who can crack any code.'

Wolff did not know any such individual.

'Really?' Jeremiah raised an eyebrow.

'He has broken into both CIA and FBI facilities on numerous occasions and never been caught,' Wolff said. This was sounding better by the moment. He should have been a writer for American television shows. 'I imagine he is like the boy, but a little more, shall we say, manageable.'

Jeremiah thought for a moment. 'Perhaps I

should have sought this individual first.'

'Perhaps,' Wolff said noncommittally. 'I would need to see the device, however, before I could make a determination.'

'Of course,' Jeremiah nodded to himself. This seemed like a good plan. He first wanted to use one of the boy's friends to make him see reason, but if that did not work then a backup plan would be available. He looked up. 'It seems our business together may not yet be finished.'

Wolff smiled and said nothing.

Chapter Twenty-Seven

Chad was ill. Very ill.

Halfway through the night I had been awoken by his cries. Then the other prisoners had started. Some of them had yelled abuse from their alcoves. Others laughed and cat called. Recoil had threatened to put Chad out of his misery. Only Drink had remained silent.

'No-one comes near him,' I yelled into the darkness. 'I'll kill anyone who tries to touch him!'

That shut them up for a while. True to form I heard Chad give a laugh.

'Hey Axel,' he said. 'You some kind of tough guy?'

'Of course,' I said. 'Don't you know that?'

'You're a dweeb,' he said faintly.

'How are you feeling?' I asked.

'What do you think?' he said.

I felt his forehead. He was burning up. Damn. This was the last thing we needed. Chad's powers were formidable. In some ways he was more powerful than me. With him out of action and my own powers liable to fail at any moment…

Well, things weren't looking good.

Getting Zachary out of here would be difficult enough without having to carry Chad out too.

'I feel hungry,' Chad said. 'How long is it since we ate?'

'About two days.'

'No wonder I feel hungry.' He whispered, 'Lean closer.'

I did. 'Yeah?'

'You know that virus has to be stopped.'

'Sure. That's why we're here.'

'I mean it's more important than anything. You know what I mean?'

Not really. 'No.'

'I'm saying you've got to get Zachary out of here and get back home. Even if that means leaving me here.'

'I'm not leaving you here.'

He gripped my arm. 'You've got to look after everyone. Including my sister.'

'Okay,' I said uncertainly.

'That doesn't mean you two can start dating.'

Okay. He wasn't too sick. He was still a pain in the ass.

'I wouldn't dream of it.'

'Why? She's not pretty enough for you?'

'Of course she's—. Look, shut up. We're both getting out of here.'

'I need food,' Chad groaned. 'I'm hungry.'

'I've got a plan for that.'

'What is it?'

'Just wait and see.'

The hours passed slowly. Every so often I would hear screams or moans in the night. I glanced at my watch. It was almost time for the lights to come on. I had a plan for getting the food and I'd already made up my mind I might have to kill someone to make this whole thing work.

So be it. Even other than Chad's life there was also the rather major issue of the Doomsday virus and the deaths of seven billion people. I had killed other people before out of necessity and I would do it again.

The lights flickered on. Both Drink and Recoil rose from their bunks and waited at the entrance to the alcove. They eagerly looked up at the ceiling. I tried to imagine what it would be like living in this place for years. It's impossible to conceive of such a thing. There was no fresh air. Food and water were luxury items. And how did someone wile away the hours and the days and the years in this place? There was no television. No books. Nothing to help pass the time.

If there was a living Hell on this Earth, this was it.

No-one deserved to be treated in this manner. No matter what crime—and probably most of the inmates here had committed no crime—they did not deserve to rot here in this terrible place.

The slots in the ceiling opened. A few seconds passed and then the food fell through. I was aware that food was dropping down through three separate slots, but I focused entirely on the slot closest. As the food fell I formed a platform, caught it and dragged it through the air toward Chad and myself.

It landed in a heap next to us. Drink made a grab for it as did Recoil, but I threw up a shield and closed them out. The cat man sprang at the barrier and bounced off. He turned around and took a swipe at Drink, but he turned to water. Recoil ran away and cowered on his bench on the other side of the enclosure.

I hate to say it, but I experienced an enormous sense of pleasure at seeing the expression of fear on Recoil's face.

I had foiled them. So far. We had a pile of food. I had learnt to never take anything for granted. Over on the other side of the enclosure I saw a life and death battle taking place between two mods. One was the thin man who was able to emit electricity from his hands. The other was someone I had not seen before; a strange half-man, half-dog looking creature with a jaw the size of a lion.

They were rolling around on the floor. Blood was spilling everywhere. I could hear screaming and yelling emanating from the human side of the jail.

Men were yelling encouragement. A thudding sound came from a darkened corner followed by a terrible groan.

I felt sick and looked away.

Chad's eyes were open again. 'Hey buddy,' he said faintly.

'Hey,' I said.

'That was good,' he said. 'Fast.'

Sweat was rolling down his face. He started to cough. Once he started, he could not seem to stop. He continued for about two minutes before he finally buried his face in his sleeve. I began to examine the pile of food I had retrieved for us. Good thing I wasn't expecting the equivalent of a three course meal, because this stuff was little more than garbage. There was half a loaf of stale bread, three apples, two oranges and a pile of goop that looked like someone had boiled vegetable skins into a mush.

The bread had patches of mold growing on it, but I broke those sections off and divided the remainder in two. I gave some to Chad and he sat up on the bench and listlessly struggled to swallow it.

After that he ate one of the apples and an orange.

Despite my hunger I found it hard eating the food. Outside of here I would have discarded all of it into the garbage without a second thought. Now I realized this meager supply of rations could mean the difference between life and death.

Chapter Twenty-Eight

Chad lay back down and went to sleep. I settled onto the bench with the remaining food and began to think. I had identified Zachary. Now we had to get out of this place. The next step had to be to work out an escape plan.

I glanced over to Drink and Recoil. They both looked rather down in the dumps. They had been here for years. Surely they had some sort of idea about escape.

'Hey guys,' I said. 'Interested in some food?'

Recoil looked at me as if I'd just said a dirty word, but Drink nodded in a friendly enough fashion. I took one of the oranges, lowered my shield momentarily and tossed it toward him. He instantly started eating it. Recoil's eyes opened wide, but he said nothing.

'Want some?' I asked.

'Sure,' he said.

I repeated the action and a moment later Recoil was hungrily biting into the apple. I waited until both men had eaten their share. They both still looked hungry—who didn't in this place—but they appeared a little less hostile.

'I want to talk strategy,' I said.

'Sure,' Drink replied.

'You're still going for the Noble Peace Prize?' Recoil asked.

'We need to get out of here,' I said.

'I hadn't thought of that,' Recoil said. 'What a great idea.'

I persisted. 'You guys have been here longer than me. How do we arrange an escape?'

A sound came from the bars separating the mods from the humans. I glanced over. It was Zachary with another man. Carefully keeping my shield in place, I went over to the bars.

'Hey,' I said.

Zachary pointed to his friend. 'This is Frank Seth. We overheard you boys talking.'

'And?'

'Frank thinks there's a way out.'

'How?'

'It's through your side,' Frank said. He was an older man. Maybe about sixty. Thin as a stick. He had a long beard down to his waist. 'Your mod friends should know about it, but we want out too.'

I wondered how to handle this. Obviously I wanted to get Zachary out, but I had to do it in such as way as to not appear obvious. We had a cover story—that we had been abandoned by our government. Maybe now was the time to use it.

'I want to get everyone out of here,' I said. 'Every single inmate.'

Zachary smirked. 'Good luck with that.'

'I'm going to make the government pay for what they did to us,' I said. 'First they wiped our memory. Then they experimented on us. Then they dumped us in here like criminals.'

I hoped I sounded bitter. It wasn't too hard, actually, because a lot of the resentment was real.

'Ask your friends about Edmund Domain,' Frank said.

Zachary nodded. 'It's probably our best bet if the story's true.'

'We'll talk later,' I said.

I returned to the cell. Fortunately my shield was holding up okay. My powers had not failed me. And a good thing too. With Chad out of action I was the only one who was still able to fight.

'Tell me about Domain,' I said to Drink and Recoil.

Recoil shrugged, but Drink started straight away.

'Domain is one of the mods,' he said. 'He has his own alcove. Apparently there's a tunnel at the back of his alcove.'

'A tunnel?' I said. 'Like out of here? So why doesn't he leave?'

'He's too large,' Recoil said. 'He can't fit through the hole.'

'You're joking.'

He shook his head. 'I'm completely serious, little one. Once you see Edmund Domain you'll see what I mean.'

'What alcove is he in?'

Recoil cast a glance at Drink. 'Information

isn't free.'

I looked down at our food and supplied each of the men with another piece of fruit each. They ate it rapidly before answering. I actually felt sad for these men. Obviously food had been whisked away from them so many times in the past, it was imperative to eat first before doing anything else.

Finally Drink finished his piece of fruit. 'Maybe he was human. Once. That was a long time ago. Now he's more like some sort of monster.'

'I don't think I've seen him yet.'

'You haven't,' Recoil said. 'He only comes out once every few weeks.'

'How does he survive?' I asked.

'Like I said,' Recoil replied. 'He comes out every few weeks to eat—'

'But how—'

'—one of us.'

It took me a moment to make sense of his words. He comes out every few weeks to eat one of us. He actually ate people. Really ate people. My mind reeled at the thought. Maybe Drink was right.

Maybe Domain wasn't a human being at all, but some kind of animal.

I shook my head. Whatever the case, he still had to be overcome. We still had to break through. But maybe this whole story about the tunnel was a fallacy. How could there actually be a tunnel leading out of this place?

I asked Drink and Recoil about it.

'There was an earthquake a few years back,' Recoil said. 'It shook the whole place up pretty bad. There was actually a breakout and a few inmates escaped. That was how Domain ended up here. When they brought him here, they didn't bring him down the stairs like everyone else. They brought him through the new tunnel.'

That sort of made sense. 'But they must have sealed the tunnel back up,' I said.

'Probably,' Recoil said. 'But it may not be as difficult getting through as all those stairs and locked steel doors.'

'So why haven't you taken on Domain?'

'Even I'm not that powerful.'

'He tried once,' Drink said.

'Once was enough,' Recoil said.

'Okay,' I said thoughtfully. 'Then tonight's the night. We're breaking out of here after the lights go out.'

'What 'we' are you talking about?' Recoil asked.

'Whoever wants to come with us,' I said. 'Tonight we're leaving this place no matter what.'

Chapter Twenty-Nine

Brodie helped to arrange the tables in the main hall for dinner. She felt annoyed and frustrated, but did her best not to show it. Jason had taken her on the tour of the inside of the complex. He had been quite thorough, but had refused to show her anything below what he referred to as 'Level D'.

'That's off limits,' he said firmly.

'What's down there?' she had asked.

'It's off limits,' he repeated and that ended all further conversation.

Now she was lifting tables and arranging chairs with the others. She felt like she had made no headway at all. They had been here for a number of days and she had still not seen Ferdy. For all she knew, he could be dead.

Ebony sidled up to her carrying a bunch of chairs.

'Hey look who's joined us,' she said.

Brodie turned around.

Dan!

'Hey!' she called.

He was on the other side of the hall. He seemed to be engaged in an animated conversation with a bunch of kids around his same age. Particularly a young girl.

He turned around, said something to the others and headed over.

'Hey Brodie! Ebony! How are you going?'

'How are we?' Ebony asked. 'More's the question, how are you? Are you feeling okay?'

'Sure,' he said. 'As good as new. I've been getting to know some of the other people here. Aren't they great?'

Brodie felt like she had fallen down a rabbit hole.

'Great?' she asked. 'Are you joking?'

Dan looked offended. 'Why? What's wrong?'

'What's wrong?' Brodie hears her voice rising. She didn't want to create a scene, so she forced a smile. 'A lot of things are wrong here. We need to find Ferdy and get out of here.'

'Sure,' Dan said, casting a glance over at the

kids he had been helping. 'I know that.'

'Have you seen Ferdy?' Ebony asked.

'No,' he said. 'Have you?'

'Have I?' Even the normally quiet Ebony looked angry. 'I wouldn't be asking you if I had. Are you okay or is there something wrong with your brain?'

'There's nothing wrong with me!' Dan snapped.

Oh no, Brodie thought.

'He's in love,' she said, letting out a long breath.

'I don't know what you're talking about,' he said.

Brodie could see this conversation going on for a really long time and not getting anywhere so she quickly explained what they had found out about the Doomsday virus and the reason for their internment.

'Are you sure?' Dan asked. 'A lot of the people here seem pretty nice.'

'They're brainwashed,' Ebony said flatly. 'And it sounds like you are too.'

Dan looked like he was about to get really angry so Brodie laid a gentle hand on his arm.

'Hey Dan,' she kept her voice level. 'I'm sure a lot of these people are nice, but there's some bad stuff going down. We'll need to work together when the time arrives. Just be careful.'

'Sure,' he agreed. 'Of course.'

She leant close to him. 'This is a dangerous place. There's an FBI guy named Ethan Craddock who's working undercover here. He might identify himself to you. Make certain you keep his identity quiet.'

'Okay,' Dan said. 'Anyway, I've got to go back now.' The girl was giving him a glance and waving him over. 'I'll talk to you later.'

He headed back over to the others.

'Love,' Brodie moaned and Ebony gave her a friendly dig in the side.

Susan, the woman who had showed them around, came over and started talking to them about the evening meal. They continued to set out tables and chairs for dinner. After the meal was completed,

Susan told them Jeremiah would be delivering one of his weekly lectures. Apparently he was going to be making some sort of announcement.

'Great,' Brodie said, trying to sound enthusiastic.

The seats were rearranged again to face a small stage at the end so everyone could sit around to listen to Jeremiah. At first the stage was empty and then some music started to be piped through the sound system.

'That's the theme music from the Superman films,' Ebony whispered to Brodie.

Oh God, Brodie thought. *That's really lame.*

When Jeremiah appeared the crowd went wild and leapt to its feet. Everyone clapped enthusiastically until he waved them back down into their seats.

'Thank you people of Sanctuary,' he said. 'But the applause should be for you. The members of this community are the courageous ones. You have stood up against the New World Order and you have triumphed.'

There was another round of applause.

Jeremiah spent the next half an hour talking about the New World Order and how the United Nations had been plotting for years against the democratic rights of the individual. It all sounded rather farfetched to Brodie. She found it hard to believe people were not more questioning about it, but the whole audience seemed enthralled.

Just before he finished speaking, Jeremiah went through a few housekeeping duties with the group. Then his face became grave.

'I also have some rather sad news,' he said. 'One of our members has unexpectedly passed away.'

A ripple of small cries went through the crowd.

'Ethan Craddock died this afternoon from natural causes,' Jeremiah continued. 'We believe it was a heart attack.'

Brodie felt her own heart give an unpleasant leap while her stomach produced enough acid to melt a spoon.

'That's—' Ebony started.

Brodie nudged her hard. She fell silent.

That's the FBI agent, Ebony had been about to say. But now he was dead. Unexpectedly. From natural causes.

My foot, Brodie thought savagely. *They realized Ethan Craddock was with the FBI and decided to kill him.*

She looked across the crowd and saw that Dan was looking back at her. His face had gone pale. He looked like the world had just landed on his head. Good. He needed a reality check. These people were maniacs and had to be treated as such.

They had to find Ferdy and get out of there.

Their lives depended on it.

Chapter Thirty

I woke up at some ungodly hour. Probably early morning. I had endured the worst night's sleep of my life. I had tried getting to bed early, but my mind had continued to turn over as I thought about the coming day.

Now I've got to face Domain, I thought. *Surely he can't be as bad as they say.*

Okay, so he eats people. Maybe he's really a nice guy.

Sure. And maybe he was actually one of the kids in The Sound of Music.

Probably not.

I nudged Chad into wakefulness. That turned out to be a feat in itself. I eventually had to drag him into an upright sitting position. Even then he looked at me blearily. His face was a lather of sweat; his hair was plastered to one side.

I explained the plan to him. He listened in silence until I finished. Then he looked away and I was shocked to see tears in his eyes.

'Axel,' he said. 'I don't think I'm going to make it.'

'You're going to make it,' I said. 'We both are. We're getting out of here together.'

'I'm afraid.'

'You're going to be okay.'

'I can barely walk,' he said. 'I'm gonna die down here.'

'He's a dead weight,' a voice hissed from the darkness. 'Leave him.'

Recoil.

'When I want your opinion, I'll ask you for it,' I whispered loudly back to him.

I heard movement in the gloom. One of the fires was still burning and Recoil's face hovered only inches from my own.

'You've got to leave him if you want to stand any chance of getting out of here,' he said. 'You've got powers. You might stand a chance. But you can't have a dead weight—'

I tried to grab his shirt, but my hand simply bounced off him. I'd forgotten about his ability to repel any attack.

'He's not a dead weight,' I said. 'He's my friend. We're all getting out of here. Together.'

Recoil stepped back a few feet. I heard him saying something to Drink. Probably complaining about me. So be it.

Chad slowly stood. He hovered uncertainly on his feet before clasping my shoulder. Once again he looked like he was about to burst into tears.

'I'll help you however I can,' he promised.

'I know you will.'

'Before we do this, I gotta say something.'

'What?'

'Thanks,' he said. 'I just want to say thanks. You should be leaving me here, but you're taking me with you. And after the hard time I've given you—'

'In a few hours time we'll be out of here,' I told him. 'And we'll laugh about all this.'

I actually couldn't think of anything less likely. I thought it more likely I'd eat off my own foot than look back on any of this experience and laugh. Still, I had to keep up Chad's spirits.

'Laugh,' he said. 'Sure.'

Okay, I hadn't fooled him either.

Drink and Recoil came over.

'You guys ready?' Drink asked.

'We're ready,' I said. 'You need to point out Domain's alcove. I'm going to go in alone and take him down. I'll give you a yell when it's safe to follow.'

They didn't say anything for a moment. Then Drink said, 'You think that's a good idea?'

I didn't bother answering that question. Instead, I said, 'I'll get the guys from the other side.'

We left the enclave. A single fire was still burning, but now it was down to embers. Someone cried out softly in the night. On the other side of the enclosure I saw someone standing in the doorway of their recess watching us. It was the guy who was able to change from human form to a gas.

He watched me without moving.

I went to the bars. Immediately Zachary came over and I focused on forming a field to bend the bars apart. I did it as quietly as possible, but it still sounded like a god damn awful racket at that time of the morning.

'Where's Frank Seth?' I asked.

'He didn't make it through the night.'

My God, I thought. *What a place.*

'What's your plan?' Zachary asked.

I explained what I intended to do.

'That Domain is some kind of monster,' he said. 'Are you sure—'

'I'm sure,' I interrupted. 'We'll be out of here before you know it.'

Returning to the others, I noticed Chad was still on his feet, but leaning badly to one side.

'Which one is Domain's alcove?' I whispered.

Both Drink and Recoil pointed to one in the middle. I had not seen anyone come or go from the enclosure during our entire time here. Now I knew why.

'I'll go in,' I said. 'When Domain is finished, I'll give you the signal.'

'What's the signal?' Chad asked.

'You'll know it when you hear it,' I said.

I went over to the fire and grabbed out a stick with one end fully alight. At least I would be able to see. I started to the alcove. Even before I reached the doorway I could smell something from the interior. It smelt bad. A rotten meat smell. I didn't want to think too much about what that would be.

I allowed my eyes to grow accustomed to the gloomy darkness. It was a large area. Bigger than I expected. It really seemed to be some sort of tunnel unlike the little I'd seen of the other enclosures. My light illuminated the floor. Sticks seemed to be strewn across the ground like the floor of a forest.

As I navigated my way around them I glanced down at one of them and saw the timber looked remarkably pale.

Oh hell, I thought. *They're not sticks. They're bones.*

They were everywhere. As my eyes became accustomed to the dark, I realized I was actually standing in the middle of hundreds of bones. My heart had already been pumping a thousand beats a minute. Now it leapt into some sort of high gear. In the back of my mind I had been thinking that the stories about Domain were actually an exaggeration. After all, no-one was really a cannibal. That's just plain stupid.

No. Domain was a cannibal.

Welcome to the twenty-first century. Cannibalism is alive and well.

Toward the back of the enclosure I spotted a section of wall darker than the rest. I hadn't seen Domain yet. Possibly this area was so large it may have contained some smaller enclaves. Maybe he was asleep in one of them. At least this darker area may have been where the tunnel ran away into the rock.

I made my way toward the tunnel. Just before I reached it I realized it seemed to dip down rather suddenly. Lowering my burning timber slightly, I missed the bone on the floor and stepped right down onto it.

The tunnel moved.

It took me all of a second to realize the tunnel I had been heading directly toward was not actually a tunnel at all, but the man/creature they called Domain. The resemblance between a human being and whatever he was remained rudimentary. He sat up and looked at me with some sort of rudimentary single eye in the middle of his forehead. He looked like some sort of yeti or Sasquatch, but built like a brick wall.

His face appeared almost human, but as if a human face had been squashed flat and the jaw lowered. This jaw dropped down now in complete surprise, revealing two rows of glistening teeth. Possibly no-one had ever entered his home without kicking and screaming for help.

Certainly no-one had come in of their own volition.

His single eye widened in surprise. He blinked twice. Focused on me and his face took on an expression of extreme rage. He wanted to kill me. Then he wanted to eat me. Worst of all, maybe he wanted to do it in the opposite order.

That's when I poked him hard in the eye with the burning stick.

Terror makes you strong. I shoved as hard as I possibly could and Domain shrieked and swatted at me. I threw up a shield and it saved me from the worse of the impact, but I still went flying.

He was on his feet in a second, and I followed up with a hurricane force wind that knocked him backwards. He hit the ground, rolled once then threw himself across the room at me. He was fast. And powerful. He aimed a punch at me, but somehow it penetrated my shield and hit me in the chest.

I slammed into the floor. As he jumped again I built a flying platform and rose up into the air. His hands raked the space under me, but he could not reach me. I focused on building up another massive hurricane blast, took a deep breath and slammed it into him.

He flew across the chamber. This time he was not so quick to rise. More wary, he slowly climbed to his feet and advanced with hate in his single, damaged eye. He wanted to kill me. He wanted to tear me limb from limb. He wanted to make me suffer for the pain I had caused him.

Which was unfortunate for me, because at that moment my powers failed and I went crashing into the floor.

Chapter Thirty-One

It had been days since I last had problems with my powers. Maybe in the back of my mind I thought the loss had simply been an aberration, a momentary failure in the neurons of my brain, a hiccup in the day to day life of a superhero.

Well, there are worse hiccups than losing your powers. One of them is losing your powers whilst in the middle of a battle with a monster who wants to tear you limb from limb.

Domain advanced toward me. I tried summoning my powers. I wanted to create another blast of air to hurl at him, but nothing would happen.

When I had hit the ground, I had landed on my feet, rolled once and was almost immediately back in a standing position. Now as he walked toward me I realized he still wanted to kill me, but he was more wary. He was confused as to why I had now decided to put myself in range of his aggression.

'I want a peaceful solution,' I said loudly, holding up a hand. 'I simply want to find a way out of here. Maybe we can all escape from here. I want us to be friends.'

The chances of us becoming friends had probably diminished dramatically when I poked him in the eye with a burning stick. Still, all I had were my words and they would have to make do.

'Do you understand what I'm saying? I want us to be friends.'

Maybe we could go out for drinks, I thought. *Possibly a game of Monopoly.*

The creature cocked his head to one side. He looked almost human for a moment. Maybe he really was considering my offer or maybe he was wondering what part of me to eat first. It was impossible to tell. I actually wondered if there was any humanity left in his head. If he ever had been human. Maybe I wasn't fighting a mod at all. Maybe Domain had always been some sort of Sasquatch creature and the North Koreans had simply confined him in Yodak Jail for fun.

He growled. Not an angry growl, but something approaching an almost human sound. Then he blinked and the sudden pain in his eye seemed to settle it. A peaceful resolution and any chance of a game of Monopoly were out of the question. He let out an unearthly roar and charged at me.

I tried to put up a shield, but nothing happened. The creature hit into me at full pelt and I literally went flying into the air. It was like being hit by a car. My head hit the floor hard. I was dazed for a few seconds. It was all Domain needed to pick me up again and hurl me across the room.

Crouching into a ball, I rolled across the floor, but at the last instant hit my elbow. Excruciating pain ran up my arm. It was so bad my entire arm went numb. It felt like my arm was broken. I stood and started to babble something to try to reason with Domain. It was pointless.

He advanced on me and now I saw a new expression in his face. A look of knowing. He now realized whatever powers I had were gone and he finally had the upper hand.

All he now had to do was deliver the death blow.

He charged at me again as I tried to bring up my shield.

Nothing happened.

It was time to die.

Except at that instant a burst of flame poured through the air and engulfed Domain in one mighty explosion. He continued toward me like a rampaging bull, but I threw myself out of the way. He flew past me, fell and hit the floor. Blinded, engulfed in fire, he rolled around as he tried to extinguish the blaze, but it was all to no avail.

I turned around to see Chad stumbling into the chamber. He fired another blast at Domain and the creature let out a last scream of rage and terror before its lungs were engulfed in flame. Then it became impossible for it to make another sound as its world was reduced to pain and oblivion and finally death.

Chad took one more single step forward before he collapsed face first into the floor.

I raced to him and tried to bring him around, but he was unconscious. The wound in his shoulder was seeping some sort of puss. We had to get out of there. We had to escape Yodak and find the plant to save him or he would die.

Footsteps sounded from behind me.

Zachary and the others were carefully entering the enclosure. I felt like making a cutting remark, but I stifled the impulse. I could hardly blame them for holding back. I certainly hadn't wanted to enter this terrible place.

'Is it over?' Drink asked hesitantly.

'It's over,' I said. 'Domain's dead. Now we need to find a way out of here.'

The whole place stunk of burnt flesh. It was sickening. I grabbed Chad in a fireman's lift, balanced him across my shoulders and followed the others toward the back of the chamber. I had been right about one thing. Where Domain had been lying asleep was a tunnel. The only problem for me was that he had been blocking it.

Recoil had another flaming torch with him. He held it aloft as we rapidly made our way down the passageway. After a moment I felt something move against my face.

Wind.

This seemed too good to be true.

Which proved to be the case after walking through the tunnel for another minute. The tunnel thinned out more and more until we were walking single file along the rift. Obviously it was little more than a crack in the earth. Zachary's story about it being caused by an earthquake seemed correct. Finally we saw the end. A thin crack in the rock that had been rather inexpertly sealed with concrete.

'There's wind on the other side,' Recoil said.

He lowered the torch and now I could see light seeping through the tiny gaps in the rock.

'We need to break through, but how are we going to do that?' Zachary asked.

'Leave this to me,' Drink said. 'That's only sandstone around the concrete and water is a powerful element. Given time it can wear mountains away to dust.'

He squeezed past Recoil and pushed his hand into the gap. It turned to water, but it did not simply remain still. In that tiny space I saw the liquid rotating around as if a mighty whirlpool were located in the tiny gap. Within seconds the gap was larger.

'Think of the Colorado river,' Drink said. 'A body of water tumbling across the countryside for millions of years until eventually you end up with the Grand Canyon. That's what I'm doing.' He continued to swirl the liquid around in the gap faster and faster. 'Millions of years of landscaping in a matter of seconds.'

The gap grew larger and larger. Within a few minutes it was large enough for someone to crawl through. Drink went first. Then Recoil. I passed Chad out to him and then Zachary with myself in the rear. We were in a thin crack in the earth. The ground beneath our feet was an uneven mound of dirt and rock. Ahead of us lay a thin crevice in the rock. We pushed through it until we found ourselves on the side of a hill. A barren landscape of scrub and rock lay ahead of us.

In the distance I could see the ocean.

We were free.

Chapter Thirty-Two

'We have a problem,' Jeremiah said. 'It's with your friend Ferdy.'

Ebony and Brodie looked at each other. They had been summonsed into Jeremiah's office a few minutes before thinking they were about to be questioned about Ethan Craddock. If the leader of the Sanctuary compound knew about their conversation with the FBI agent, he gave no indication. Instead, he seemed almost conciliatory.

'What sort of problem?' Brodie asked.

'Your friend Ferdy will not cooperate,' Jeremiah said carefully. 'As you are well aware, as much as he is a genius—and he is one of unparalleled abilities—he also suffers from some defects in communication. He does not understand what is at stake.'

Maybe he does, Brodie thought. *Maybe he understands all too well.*

'So what do you want from us?' Ebony asked.

'I want you to speak to him,' Jeremiah said. 'I

want you to encourage him to break the Barricade code.'

'Why would we do that?' Brodie asked. 'You want to kill everyone on Earth and you want our help to do that. Why would we help you?'

'Think of it as buying time for yourselves,' Jeremiah said smoothly. 'You may all continue to live for as long as you are prepared to be part of our family.' He spread his hands. 'We want you to be part of our glorious future in the New Era. I know Jason has taken quite a liking to you, Brodie.'

'So I understand,' she said.

'You will be married,' Jeremiah said. 'As will you, Ebony. There is another boy who has expressed interest in becoming your husband.'

Brodie cast a glance at Ebony. Whatever the quiet girl thought of her impending marriage to a complete stranger, she kept to herself.

'That is the future that lies ahead for you now,' Jeremiah said.

Brodie was thinking along quite different lines. She was thinking about taking this whole scenario in a brand new direction, starting with ripping off one of Jeremiah's arms and beating him with it until he took her to Ferdy. Then she would grab the virus and get all of them out of this crazy house.

It all seemed like a plan until Jeremiah turned on the monitor on his desk.

'We have another means of persuasion,' he said.

The monitor flickered to life. It took Brodie a moment to understand what she was looking at. It was a room and in the room was what appeared to be a table. On the table was—

'Dan!' Ebony cried. 'What are you doing to him?'

'Nothing,' Jeremiah said. 'Yet.'

Dan lay on the contraption. Jeremiah and his people had been quite clever in building the contraption out of timber. Dan's powers could only be used against metal. As they stared in horror at the device, they realized it was a rack, a medieval torture device used to stretch a person until their limbs dislocated from each other and their body was torn apart.

Ebony felt sick. She swallowed hard and tasted vomit in her mouth.

'Leave him alone,' she said, but her voice sounded distant in the small room. 'You people are monsters. You—'

She wanted to reach across the table and touch Jeremiah and turn him to oxygen or carbon or granite and then he would be finished. But the people stationed next to the rack would start to turn the wheels on the rack and how quickly could they stop them?

Not quickly enough.

'I'll help you,' Ebony said.

'Ebony!' Brodie said. 'No! You can't—'

Ebony turned on her. 'Shut up!'

Brodie had never seen such a look of dismay and rage on the quiet girl's face. She looked like she wanted to kill someone. Brodie could understand the sensation. Right now she wanted to put Jeremiah on that rack so he could get a feeling of what it would be like to be so completely helpless.

'Okay,' Brodie said. 'We'll help you.'

'I'll speak to Ferdy,' Ebony said with tears in her eyes. 'I can get through to him.'

Jeremiah raised an eyebrow. 'Wouldn't it be better if both you girls—'

'No,' Brodie interrupted. 'Ebony is closer to Ferdy than I am. She can get through to him if anyone can.'

Jeremiah seemed to accept the explanation. 'Then let's get started.' He pushed an intercom button on his desk and an assistant came in and Brodie was led out of the room and back to the common area. Ebony found herself being taken down a winding corridor deep into the earth. She longed to cause Jeremiah some terrible pain, but that had to wait. Now she had to cooperate and convince Ferdy to help these maniacs.

They arrived at a metal door. Jeremiah entered a code and the door swung open. They stepped through and Ebony found herself in a large chamber with paintings on the walls. Ebony was relieved to see it was a pleasant room with wildflowers in vases. It contained a bed and a table and chair.

Ferdy was sitting quietly at the table. His eyes lit up when he saw Ebony.

'Ebony!' he said, rising to his feet and running toward her.

Ebony gave him a hug.

'Not too tight,' she had to remind Ferdy.

Not only did Ferdy have an incredible brain, but he also had super strength. He could lift a car without raising a sweat. He could probably punch the door down that had locked him in here, but he was unable to work that out for himself.

'Ferdy loves you,' Ferdy said.

Ebony realized tears were running down her cheeks. 'I love you too Ferdy,' she said. 'And I've missed you.'

She looked around and realized for the first time that a pair of handcuffs, broken in two, lay on the floor nearby.

'Did you try to restrain him?' she turned to Jeremiah in fury.

He raised a hand. 'I'm sorry,' he said. 'I really am, but he would not cooperate with us. As long as you help us now we can all be friends.' He peered at Ferdy. 'You want that, don't you Ferdy?'

Ferdy looked like he would rather be friends with a brick than with Jeremiah. He glanced over at Ebony.

'My friend is Ebony,' he said. 'Shall I compare thee to a summer's day? Thou are more lovely and more temperate.'

'I think that's Shakespeare,' Ebony said.

'The eighteenth sonnet,' Ferdy said. 'Shakespeare lived from 1564 and died in 1616.'

'Thanks Ferdy,' Ebony said.

'I'm going to get Barricade for us,' Jeremiah said. 'In the meantime, I hope you can make Ferdy see reason.'

Jeremiah left the room. Ebony asked Ferdy if he was okay and if he had been eating all right. It seemed the Sanctuary people had been feeding him, but had not been giving him chocolate which was his favorite food.

'Ebony, friend,' he said. 'Do you have chocolate?'

'I don't have any,' she said.

'Chocolate is made from cocoa,' he said.

'I know,' she said, looking around the room. She hated this place. She hated Jeremiah. He had locked poor Ferdy in this place and treated him like some sort of criminal. How could someone treat a harmless person like Ferdy with anything less than love and compassion?

She was just wondering this when Jeremiah returned. He had a long, metal tube in his hand about three feet in length. A digital display ran along one side of it with a keyboard set into the metal below it. Jeremiah laid it on the table before them.

Ebony looked down at the display. A meaningless row of letters and numbers filled the display.

'E794GB5…' her voice trailed off.

'I've shown this to Ferdy before, but he just looks at it without comprehension,' Jeremiah said. 'This is the Barricade device. The display is the code that I want your friend Ferdy to crack for me. If he doesn't, then young Dan is going to be sorry.'

'Dan,' Ferdy said. 'Dan is one of Ferdy's friends.'

'That's right,' Jeremiah said. 'One of Ferdy's friends is going to suffer.'

Chapter Thirty-Three

We continued toward the sea. I told the group we had a sophisticated aircraft waiting on the shoreline for us. Some friends had arranged to supply it for us in case an escape became available. After about a mile, Recoil bade us farewell and wished us luck. Considering he would have happily killed us the previous day for a piece of moldy bread, his farewell was surprisingly good natured.

He followed a ravine away from us. We didn't see him again.

Zachary pointed to a plant growing on a hillside.

'That's the plant your friend needs,' he said. 'He needs to eat it as well as applying it directly to the wound.'

I broke off a piece of the plant and used a makeshift rock and pestle to crush it. After a few minutes I had a sizeable quantity. I divided it in half and combined some with water seeping through a crack in a rock face. I tried feeding the mixture to

Chad, but he could barely swallow.

'I'll put some in the wound,' Zachary said.

While he smeared it across the cuts in Chad's shoulder, I wondered if we may have already been too late. He was very pale. His fever had broken and now his breathing was shallow.

'Come on Chad,' I said. 'Don't give up now.'

I tried feeding some of the liquid to him. He started to cough and I stopped.

'Just a little at a time,' Drink said, looking around.

I could understand his concern. We were in a tiny valley. No-one was around, but that could change in seconds.

'We'd better keep moving,' Zachary suggested.

I nodded. I forced some more of the mixture down Chad's throat. Despite his coughing, it seemed like some of it was staying down. We half carried, half dragged Chad between us down the valley. A humid wind poured across the valley; I could smell the sea. I had already felt a strange impulse in my arm. It was where the chip had been inserted. Almost like a compass pointing north, I knew the invisible craft was located on the coast to our left.

The valley flattened out. Now we could see some farm houses on both sides. There was a family doing some work outside one of the houses.

Taking refuge behind a ridge, we surveyed the farmers. We needed to keep moving. It was still early morning, but I didn't know how long it would take before the authorities realized there had been a jail break. Possibly the other prisoners might realize an avenue of escape had been opened up and they might break out. There could be a mass jail break. I wasn't too sure how I felt about that. Some of the prisoners were obviously dangerous, but many of them were probably innocent men. I supposed there was nothing I could do about it, so I pushed it from my mind.

I felt our escape plane was close by. Maybe only a couple of miles. We had to keep moving.

'What about your powers?' Drink asked, peering over at the farmers. 'Can you use them to get us to your ship?'

'They're a bit depleted right now,' I said. I didn't want to say they were completely inoperative. 'We need to do this on our own.'

'I say we go,' Zachary said. 'Most people in North Korea will mind their own business. This is a government controlled state. Raising a fuss over seeing strange people in a field may not be in their best interest.'

'You're probably right,' Drink agreed.

We started across the field. By the halfway point we noticed the people at the farmhouse had stopped and were watching us. They did not wave or show any interest in communicating with us. Neither did we. Keeping on a straight line, we reached the end of the field where it met a tarred road.

Crossing over, we started across another field. This one dipped down to meet with the shore. I felt the strong pull of the GPS device as it seemed to pull us across the field.

'We're almost there,' I gasped. Chad was getting heavier by the moment.

'I think I can hear an engine,' Drink said.

We paused momentarily. A truck was coming around a bend and heading down the road. We heard the screech of its brakes as we continued across the field. Now the low-lying plant life and dirt gave way to gravel.

A shot rang out.

'Hell!' Zachary said.

We hurried down an embankment and out of sight as a bullet pinged off a rock to our left.

'There it is!' I cried.

A modern looking fighter craft sat on the beach.

'Where?' Drink asked.

He couldn't see it. 'Don't worry,' I said. 'It's there.'

We hurried across the rocky beach as quickly as we could, but it was slow going. Chad seemed to be getting heavier by the moment. Now the craft lay less than fifty feet away. More shots rang out and bullets ricocheted off the rocks around us. I tried forming a shield around us and nothing happened.

Damn!

'Take him!' I commanded.

Zachary and Drink grabbed Chad. I focused again on trying to get a shield up, but my powers were gone. Just as we reached the craft I saw the plane shimmer slightly. Zachary and Drink gasped in amazement. Obviously they could see it too.

A hatch opened automatically on the side. Bullets were flying everywhere now. Drink climbed in. I followed after him as Zachary helped to struggle Chad into the aircraft. As the hatch swung shut behind us, Zachary cried out in pain.

He and Chad fell to the floor.

'I'm shot,' he said, grabbing his leg.

'Get us out of here!' Drink yelled. 'I'll look after them!'

Getting us to the ship seemed to be the easy part. Now I had to work out how it worked. I climbed into the flight cabin.

'What the hell do I do?' I muttered.

'Flex fighter online,' the computer announced and the display came to life.

'Flex?' I said.

'Enter audio input,' it said.

'We need to get out of here,' I said.

'Destination?'

'We need to get back to the United States.'

'Destination inputted.'

I felt the craft lift off the ground with a mighty roar. I fell sideways as it rose up into the air. Bullets were striking the side of the ship, but it seemed to be dealing with the attack with no problems. It surged forward and upward.

Looking through a window, I saw the North Korean mainland fall away behind us.

'Yes!' I said, punching the air.

Now I had to make certain Zachary and Chad were okay. The others were in the main compartment. As I entered, I saw Chad on one of the seats. He had been strapped in. His eyes were slightly open and he was looking around in a confused manner.

'How did we end up here?' he asked. 'Where's the jail?'

'We escaped,' I told him. 'We—'

I didn't get any further. At that moment I

glanced at the others. Drink was strapped into one of the seats as well, but the person sitting next to him was not Zachary. It was a girl looking at me with a grimace of pain on her face. A ragged bandage was wrapped around her leg.

My mouth dropped open. 'What—? Where on earth—?'

'I'm sorry,' the girl said. 'My name is Cecelia.'

'Where's Zachary?' I looked around in amazement.

'I'm a shape shifter,' Cecelia said. 'Zachary's been dead for nine months and I've been taking his place.'

Chapter Thirty-Four

Ferdy liked puzzles. He looked into Ebony's face and saw two blue eyes. A nose. A mouth. Blonde hair. Her face was a type of puzzle. It was hard for him to focus on all its features at the same time, but he knew when he put it all together it made up the person he knew as Ebony.

'Ebony,' he said.

'That's right, Ferdy,' she said. 'I'm Ebony and I need you to open this cylinder for me. It's a code. A cipher.'

Ferdy looked down at the cylinder. He saw the rows of numbers and letters.

'E794...' his voice trailed off.

'What does it mean?' Ebony asked. 'Can you tell me?'

Ferdy looked into her face again. The man next to her was named Jeremiah. Ferdy didn't like Jeremiah. He was a bad man and he had known a few bad people. The first bad people had been back at the place they called The Agency. There was a time before The Agency. Ferdy could remember snippets of it. A man and a woman. His parents. A brother and sister.

There had been a car accident and after the accident he could not remember seeing them again. He remembered doctors and he remembered one of them quite clearly.

'This will not hurt,' the doctor said.

But the doctor had lied. It had hurt. A lot. After the drugs had taken hold his teeth had clenched together and he had almost bitten through his tongue. After that the doctors had placed a piece of rubber between his teeth.

When he had awoken the world had become both very small and very large at the same time. It was very small because he could only focus on one thing at a time. An entire human face was too complex. Too confusing. In comparison, math's problems or books were simple things. He could read them and understand them immediately because he could see them all at once. They were easy.

Ferdy knew the entire periodic table of

elements. He could recite them forwards or backwards or tell anyone that Rhodium's atomic number was forty-five and its atomic weight was 102.905.

It was discovered in 1803 by a man named Wollaston. Usually when he told people information like this—even his friends—they often interrupted him or ignored him. People missed out on a lot of things. Sometimes they were stupid. Even his friends could be stupid, but that did not mean he did not like them. He liked them a lot.

Like Ebony. She was his best friend and she paid him the most attention out of anyone. Like right now as she stared into his eyes and said, 'Ferdy, you need to listen to me. You need to open this cylinder. You need to crack this code.'

'A cylinder is a three dimensional geometric shape,' he said. 'Its area is twice pi times r times h where r stands for radius and—'

'That's right,' Ebony said. 'But we need to work out this cipher. Do you understand? We need to work this out or Dan is going to be hurt.'

Dan played computer games with Ferdy and they had fun. He was another friend.

'Cipher,' Ferdy said. 'In early times it meant zero. Now it's an algorithm used to perform either encryption or decryption.' He stopped. His stomach was making a strange sound. It was hard to focus on so many things at once. 'Ferdy needs chocolate.'

Jeremiah looked quite annoyed when he said this, but Ebony almost smiled. Almost. The expression on her face was something between a smile and looking sad.

'Ebony looks sad,' Ferdy said. Then he continued. 'The Dorabella Cipher is one of the world's most famous ciphers. It was developed by Edward Elgar to amuse his friend Dora Penny.'

'Ferdy—' Ebony began.

'Ferdy solved it last Tuesday. What a funny thing for Mr. Elgar to say to Miss Penny. Who would imagine he would say—'

'Ferdy,' Ebony interrupted him again.

He looked at her. He saw her eyes, her mouth, her lips, her hairline. He thought about quoting

Shakespeare again to her, but realized she was pointing at the metal tube.

'Can you solve this?' she asked.

He looked at the numbers and letters.

He laughed.

'So funny,' he said.

'What is?' Jeremiah asked.

Ferdy glared at him. He would not answer Jeremiah because he was a bad man.

'What's so funny?' Ebony asked.

'A substitution cipher,' Ferdy said. 'Ferdy likes substitution ciphers.'

Jeremiah looked very serious now. He was staring quite intensely at Ferdy as was Ebony. Ferdy looked at them both and then he looked at the string of letters and numbers and now he started to recall the many books he had read.

There were literally millions of them. He could read an entire book in three minutes on an ebook reader. Some days he read hundreds and hundreds of them. That was not including all the books he read during his early days at The Agency.

He thought about all those books and he started to substitute letters and numbers and they were all like the colors of a rainbow. The books did not line up together. Rather they lay on top of one another and he could see through them all at the same time.

All those books.

There were the Adventures of Huckleberry Finn and The Bible and a book about the lifecycle of woodpeckers and other books about music and now the letters were flowing like the water in a river.

'You can't step into the same river twice,' he said gravely.

He was checking on how seats were laid out in commercial airplanes and the works of T. S Eliot and how they looked represented in Morse Code and the birthdates of thousands of famous people and a list of all the known stars and planets.

He laughed. 'Pluto isn't a planet anymore.'

It was all coming together now and that's how he liked it. He was Ferdy and Ebony was his friend and she had asked him to work out the code. He was reading through the Washington Phone book and checking lines of longitude and latitude and checking the population growth for the countries of the world.

He reached out with a hand and started pushing buttons on the keypad.

'So simple,' he said. 'Stephen Hawking was born on the eighth of January in nineteen forty-two.'

Ebony and Jeremiah stared at him in silence as he continued to push buttons. Finally he hit the enter key and the Doomsday device clicked. It slid open to reveal two vials filled with a pale blue liquid.

'Ferdy still likes chocolate,' he said.

Chapter Thirty-Five

'But I know everything Zachary knew,' Cecelia said.

I felt ill in my stomach. 'Such as?'

It was a terrible shock to realize that the person we had thought was Zachary Stead was actually an eighteen year old girl named Cecelia Watson. I couldn't believe the person we had just helped escape from Yodak jail had taken his place. It didn't seem possible. Yet here she was sitting in front of us, bleeding all over the floor.

'I'm a shape shifter,' she said. 'But I'm only able to do it for people I'm with at the time of their death.'

'So where is the Sanctuary Compound?' I asked.

'Why do you want to know?'

'That's my business. Where is the compound?'

'I'm happy to tell you,' Cecelia said. 'But then I want to be allowed to go on my way.'

'After we make certain that what you've told us is the truth,' I said. 'Then you can go.'

'I'm not satisfied with that,' she said.

'You'll have to be.'

A beeping sound came from the console on the flight deck. I entered the room and slid the door shut behind me. A voice came over the speaker.

'This is Palmer,' the voice said. 'Do you read me? Over.'

Agent Palmer had told us before we left that she would use her surname in any communications in case anyone else—like Zachary or Cecelia Watson—was listening. I peered down at the console. A lesson in how to work this thing might have been handy.

I put on the headphones and manipulated the microphone. After a few faulty attempts I had a successful conversation underway and explained the situation.

'Get Zachary—or Cecelia—or whatever she calls herself to pinpoint the location of the compound on the flight display,' she said.

'Uh, roger that,' I said.

I brought Cecelia onto the flight deck. She spent the next few minutes studying a swipe map on one of the display consoles. Finally she pinpointed an area in Montana. I kicked her out of the room and opened up the line again to Agent Palmer.

'I can see the area she's pinpointed on your display,' she responded. 'We'll have agents move in immediately.'

'What's happening with Brodie and the others,' I asked. 'Have you heard from them?'

'Negative,' she said. 'We'll see you at the compound.'

The line went dead.

I sat back in the flight seat as the Flex plane soared across the sky. There seemed little to do after that. According to Agent Palmer it was going to take us around ten hours to reach the site. While there were no beds on the plane, the seats were quite comfortable. I applied more of the plant to Chad's wounds and forced a little more of the mixture down his throat.

With Drink's help I tightly applied a fresh

bandage to Cecelia's leg. Fortunately she had only suffered a flesh wound, but she still looked pale. She dozed off and I turned my attention to Chad.

His color had improved a lot. The cut on his shoulder seemed to be drying out. While I examined it he opened his eyes and seemed to recognize me for the first time in hours.

'Hey, is that you, Axel?' he asked.

'It's me?'

'I don't remember you being so ugly.'

He was sounding better already.

'I've always been this ugly,' I said cheerfully. 'You've always been the good looking guy.'

'That's how I remember it.' He looked past me at Cecelia. 'Who's the beautiful girl?'

'Oh, you've already met her.'

'Really.'

'That's Zachary,' I said.

'Really?' he said. 'I think I'm going back to sleep.'

And he did.

I returned to the control area and examined the

flight controls. This was truly an amazing piece of technology. The controls were a series of touch screens. I didn't dare touch anything, but I made a mental note to ask for lessons after this whole situation was over.

I remembered the promise Chad and I had made to The Agency.

Well, I thought. *If we work with The Agency I might learn how to fly this thing. And a whole lot more.*

I returned to the passenger area and slumped into one of the seats. The Agency might not even want me working with them. After all, it seemed my powers were fading. Probably the others would remain with the organization. At least The Agency would want Chad. His powers were still fully intact.

Closing my eyes, it seemed like only seconds, but suddenly I awoke. The sound of the engines was changing. Much to my amazement, Chad was up on his feet and looking out the window.

'How you going, partner?' I asked.

'Better,' he said. 'Much better. It looks like

this thing is coming in to land.'

'Really?'

He nodded. 'And not a moment too soon for sleeping beauty. She's looking as bad as I felt.'

I went over and touched her arm. Cecelia felt cold and clammy. Her face was pale. She looked up at me through half opened eyes.

'Are we there yet?' she asked.

It was Chad who answered. 'We are. And there's a whole welcoming party waiting for us.'

I looked over his shoulder and saw a forest below us. Helicopters and vehicles were parked all through the woodland. Through some miracle of automatic flying, the Flex was able to find a relatively empty area and make a landing.

We climbed out and I breathed in the scent of the Montana wilderness. Wow. I felt like falling to my knees and kissing the earth. Home. Dorothy was right when she said there was no place like it.

I climbed out first, assisting Chad down the ladder. Drink followed next and lingered behind us. A group of people appeared through the trees and made their way through the forest toward us. Agent Palmer was in the lead.

'Well done, guys,' she said. 'You've really broken open this case.'

'Thanks,' I said. 'We couldn't have done it without Drink and Zachary-Cecelia.'

'Drink?' she said.

I turned around. Drink was gone. The agents checked the plane and the surrounding area. He was not to be found. It looked like he had used the opportunity to escape.

A man of few words, I thought.

Agency personnel carried the now unconscious body of Cecelia from the plane while Agent Palmer took us toward the compound. No sooner had I asked the agent about our friends than a group of people came into sight.

Brodie. Ebony. Dan. Ferdy.

Yes!

It was a wild reunion, but it only last a few minutes. Agent Palmer came back to us with a frown on her face.

'We've got a problem,' she said. 'A big problem.'

'What is it?' I asked.

'We've got Jeremiah and all the other members of the compound,' she said. 'But we can't find the Doomsday virus.'

'Ferdy opened the canister for Jeremiah,' Ebony said in a hushed voice. She looked at everyone as if expecting them to jump down her throat. 'If he hadn't done it, then—'

'That doesn't matter now,' Palmer interrupted. 'We think someone has stolen the virus samples.'

'Who?' Brodie asked.

'It's a man with whom you're already familiar,' she said. 'His name is Solomon Wolff.'

Chapter Thirty-Six

'What?' I said in amazement. 'How is that possible?'

'Wolff was fundamental in obtaining the virus for Jeremiah,' the agent explained. 'We believe he left the area only a few minutes before we arrived.'

'Can we follow him?' Brodie asked.

'We're attempting to do that as we speak,' Palmer said. 'The whole area is surrounded. We might get lucky.'

But unfortunately as the day wore on, it became apparent that Wolff had slipped through the net. Several other law enforcement agencies turned up over the course of the afternoon—FBI, CIA and Homeland Security. I had never seen so many people in suits in the one place at the same time.

It looked pretty odd, if you want to know the truth. Don't forget, we were in the middle of the Montana wilderness. A person running about in a forest wearing a suit looks strange no matter how you look at it.

After a number of hours Agent Palmer came back to us to report what they had discovered. We were sitting in one of the many meeting rooms located within the Sanctuary Compound.

'That guy Wolff is good,' she said. 'He's been a thorn in the side of government agencies for years.'

'So you haven't been able to track him down?' Brodie asked.

'I didn't say that,' she said. 'Most of his business is conducted via disposable cell phones and he made two calls prior to leaving the compound. We've been able to trace them.'

'How?' Dan asked. 'I thought you couldn't trace cell phones.'

'Cell phone calls are routed through phone towers,' she explained. 'The local tower has a record of the destination numbers.'

'Which are?' I asked.

'There are two locations. One is in Alaska. The other is Paris,' she said. 'We'll be leaving immediately.'

'I bags Paris,' Chad said. 'I need the climate.'

I rolled my eyes. Chad was back to his old self.

'Actually we will be involving your group,' Agent Palmer said. 'The good news we don't believe Wolff intends to use the virus.'

'That is good news,' Ebony said.

I glanced over at her. She had looked downcast all afternoon. She was obviously feeling depressed and guilty over encouraging Ferdy to unlock the Barricade code. Under the circumstances, however, it was completely understandable.

'Wolff is a mercenary, but ultimately he's a businessman,' Palmer said. 'Unlike the fanatics in the Sanctuary Compound who were actually interested in Global destruction, he is only interested in making money.'

'So how does he do that?' I asked.

'Blackmail. Simply by threatening to release the viruses, he will extort money from governments. He could do it for years.'

'It's like that MAD scenario,' Dan said. 'Um…'

'Mutually assured destruction,' Ferdy said. 'Where two opposing military forces are assured of mutual destruction if they ever unleash their might. First attributed to author Wilkie Collins—'

'That's good, Ferdy,' Brodie interrupted. 'I think I get the idea.'

'Anyway,' Palmer said. 'It's time we got moving. We need to break into two groups. I suggest Axel, Ferdy and Ebony form one group. Chad, Brodie and Dan form the other.'

I don't know how everyone felt about being ordered around, but there didn't seem to be time to argue about it all. Agent Palmer jumped up and herded everyone out of the room. I had all of a minute to catch up with Brodie.

'You didn't get a chance to tell me about Sanctuary,' I said as we hurried down the corridor.

'Not much to tell.' She shrugged. 'Almost got married.'

'Uh, right,' I said.

'No, really,' she said brightly. 'I almost got married. I was asked by Jason, the son of the crazy running the place.'

'Lucky you.' I could feel my neck turning red. 'So what did you say?'

'I said I'd think about it,' Brodie replied. 'What do you think I said?'

How would I know? By this time Chad had raised an eyebrow and was trying to hide a smirk on his lips. I glared at him. Why did I save that guy? I should have left him back in Yodak jail.

'This is Agent Peterson,' Palmer said. 'He will take Axel's group. I'll take Brodie's group.'

'Uh, that's Chad's group,' Chad said.

'Sure, Chad,' Agent Palmer stared at him. 'I'll take Mr Magnifico Chad's Most Glorious Super Heroic Avenger Justice Hyper Group.'

It's not often that Chad is stuck for words. This was one of those times.

'Okay,' he finally said.

We were all still laughing when we boarded our planes.

Chapter Thirty-Seven

'Paris,' I said. 'Here we come.'

Half a day had passed since leaving Montana. I was already missing the others. Especially Brodie. I was glad she was safe, especially after her ordeal in the Sanctuary compound, but it felt like months had passed since we had last seen each other.

And almost married?

I didn't want to go there.

The plane we traveled in was similar to the Flex Fighter, but it was larger. Agent Peterson turned out to be a large well built man who looked like he spent his spare time bench pressing refrigerators and eating planks of wood for fun. He had little to say until we had almost reached Paris.

'No offense,' he said. 'But I should let you know I'm not keen to include you kids on these kinds of missions.'

'None taken,' I said. If I had a choice I'd rather be sitting in a living room somewhere watching television or playing a computer game.

'We have trained agents all over the world who can deal with these sorts of situations,' he continued. 'I know you kids have got powers—'

'Agent Orange was a defoliant and herbicide used during the Vietnam War,' Ferdy said. 'It caused birth defects.'

'That's right,' Ebony said. She was sitting next to Ferdy and gave him a brief squeeze on his shoulder.

It seemed that Peterson had lapsed to silence, so I went back and slumped next to Ebony.

Ferdy smiled. 'Ferdy is glad to be back with Ebony and Axel. They are my friends.'

'We are your friends,' Ebony said.

'Cicero said friendship makes prosperity more shining,' Ferdy said. 'And lessens diversity by dividing and sharing it.'

Ferdy—and Cicero—were right. I sat there and thought about Ferdy and the other members of our group. They were my family. I still had no memory of my past prior to being used as a guinea pig by The Agency. I had been told I had a brother.

Somewhere. I wondered what he was doing—if he existed at all.

I closed my eyes. When I opened them again Ebony gave me a smile. I had fallen asleep on her shoulder.

'Hey sleepyhead,' she said. 'Rise and shine.'

'Sorry,' I said.

'That's okay. Ferdy does that sometimes too.'

The Flex plane was coming in to land at Charles de Gaulle airport. Once it had come to a halt we disembarked and made our way to a waiting car. Peterson climbed behind the wheel and took us out onto the highway.

Less than an hour later we were coming into the heart of Paris. I had never been to Paris—not that I could remember anyway. It looked like an old city. A beautiful place. Perfect weather. Grand buildings were everywhere. French flags hung from rooftops and balconies all over the place.

'There's the Eiffel tower,' Ebony pointed.

Wow. She was right. It was one thing to see it on television and quite another to see it in person.

Even at a distance it still looked like a graceful structure. We all piled over to one side of the car.

'There'll be time for sightseeing later,' Peterson growled. 'Right now we need to focus on taking down Wolff.'

Okay, I thought. *We'll check out the sights later.*

'Where are we going?' I asked.

'He placed a call to the Hotel le Bristol. It's one of the best hotels in Paris. If we're lucky he might be at the hotel. If we're unlucky, he may have already passed the virus on to someone else for safekeeping.'

We passed an amazing looking walled structure with guards out the front.

'That's the Elysee Palace,' Peterson said.

'I thought we were leaving the sightseeing till later,' Ebony pointed out.

'Uh…well…' Peterson looked a little embarrassed.

We pulled up outside the hotel a few minutes later. It was a beautiful looking building about six stories high. Flower boxes lined the windows at street level. A curved black and gold awning covered the entry way.

Entering the lobby, we followed Peterson as he went straight to the front desk and flashed an ID card. He spoke to the hotel clerk in fluent French. After a rapid conversation, he turned back to us.

'We're in luck,' he said. 'A man by the description of Wolff checked in here only a few hours ago. Apparently he left the hotel just before we entered.'

We quickly raced out to the sidewalk. Ferdy seemed to be engaged in looking up at the sky until I quickly explained we were looking for Wolff. We all began scanning the street. Peterson and Ferdy had never encountered Wolff, but they had seen pictures of him. Ebony and I had met him once already.

Once was enough.

'General Solomon Wolff,' Ferdy said, peering down the street. 'A bad man.'

'That's right,' I said. 'We're looking for General Wolff.'

'General Solomon Wolff,' he repeated.

Ebony stared down Ferdy's line of sight. 'Down there,' she pointed. 'Ferdy's spotted him.'

A figure was sedately making his way down the sidewalk. He glanced sideways into a store window.

'That's him,' I said. 'Come on.'

Chapter Thirty-Eight

After some of the tricks Chad had pulled with his ability to produce snow, Brodie thought she'd seen enough to last a lifetime, but even she had to admit she was impressed as they flew into the airport in Alaska. They passed over Prince William Sound, a huge body of water dotted with islands. It was the most beautiful view she had ever seen.

'We're coming into Pioneer Field,' Agent Palmer said from her position in the Flex flight deck.

The airfield had a single landing strip. It was nestled between hills not far from the water. Cross winds buffeted the jet as it came into land. They stepped out onto the runway. From here they looked out at snow capped hills.

'I spotted a town on the way in,' Chad said.

'That's the city of Valdez,' Palmer explained. She explained the city had been moved after an earthquake in the nineteen sixties.

'Let's hope we don't have another one now,' Brodie said.

'An earthquake is the least of our problems,' she replied.

A car was waiting for them at the edge of the field. As they drove toward town, Palmer explained that one of Wolff's calls had been traced to a hotel, the Best Western in the heart of the city.

'It's right on the water,' she said. 'We may find Wolff here or it may be one of his operatives.'

'What's our best course of action?' Dan asked.

'We'll check at the hotel first,' Palmer said. 'The local police have been informed about Wolff and told to meet us there.'

When they arrived at the hotel to find a police officer in the lobby. He gave them a brief rundown of what he had discovered.

'It appears your man arrived here a few hours ago,' he said. 'After checking in he almost immediately headed out again.'

'Any idea where he went?' Palmer asked.

The officer shook his head. 'No. I can start asking around town if you want.'

'We might take you up on that, but let us check his room first.'

The girl at the desk handed over a key and they followed Agent Palmer up to a room on the first floor.

'I can handle this,' Chad said as they approached the room.

'Really?' Agent Palmer queried.

'Sure,' he said. 'I'll just blast Wolff if he tries anything.'

She placed a firm hand on Chad's shoulder. 'Listen buddy. We're talking about a deadly virus that can destroy every human on Earth. There's no blasting without my orders. Got that?'

'Uh, okay,' Chad said, chastised. 'No blasting.'

Palmer motioned them to one side of the door. She drew her weapon, knocked and waited a few seconds.

'Room service,' she announced.

There was no response.

She tried the key, opened the door and quickly

went inside with the others following. The interior of the hotel was empty. Extremely empty. As Brodie and the others looked about they didn't even see a bag.

'I don't think he's even been here,' Dan said, glancing in the bathroom.

'I think he looked at the local tourist directory,' Brodie said.

They grouped around the booklet. It lay askew from the other brochures provided by the hotel about local attractions. It had been opened to one of the pages.

'Maybe he was looking for something in here,' Brodie said. 'Maybe a map.'

The page showed a drawing of the local area.

'Surely he'd have Google maps on his phone,' Chad said.

'Probably,' Palmer said. 'But he may have been double checking just to be certain.' She glanced around. 'I don't think we can find out anything more here.'

They left the hotel and gathered in the parking lot.

'What do we do now?' Brodie asked. She felt cold and tired. Even though this city was fairly small, trying to find a single person felt like looking for a needle in a haystack. The Alaskan wilderness lay all around them and seemed to go on forever.

'He can't have gotten far on foot,' Palmer said. 'We'll try the local car hire companies to see if he's hired a vehicle.'

There were two hire car companies in town. Agent Palmer said she would take the vehicle to check one of them while Brodie and Dan checked the other company. She handed Brodie an ID card with her photo on it. Brodie looked down at it in amazement. It identified her as an FBI agent.

'This is so cool,' she said. 'But why the FBI?'

'Obviously most people are not familiar with The Agency,' Palmer explained.

'Where's mine?' Dan asked.

She looked down at him. 'No-one in a million years is going to think you're old enough to be an FBI agent.'

Chad looked like he was about to speak.

The agent cut him off. 'Don't even say it.'

Chad clamped his mouth shut.

Before they split up, the agent handed each of them a cell phone. 'Ring if you find anything out.'

Brodie and Dan followed a road up toward the Valdez Medical center. The town was very flat with all the buildings well spaced apart from each other. Obviously lack of room was not an issue here. Brodie noticed Dan staring at the hills surrounding the town.

'Try to stay focused,' she said, aware that she was sounding a lot like Agent Palmer. 'We need to keep an eye out for Wolff.'

She had to admit, though, the scenery was magnificent. They followed the road until they reached a small car hire place on the left hand side. It looked like it doubled as a general store as well. A bell tingled on the door as they entered. A small, friendly looking older woman looked up from the counter. Her name badge identified her as Sharon.

'Can I help you?' she asked.

Brodie produced the identification and Sharon looked suitably impressed.

'We're looking for this man,' Brodie showed her the photo of Wolff. 'Have you seen him?'

'Yes, I have. He hired a car from here about an hour ago.'

'Do you know where he went?' Dan asked excitedly.

Sharon looked at him strangely. 'Aren't you a little young to be with the FBI?'

'He's my brother,' Brodie said, then remembered that she had an Australian accent and Dan was of Chinese origin. 'My half-brother. I'm minding him while I'm on this case.'

It all sounded rather lame to her, but it was the best she could do under the circumstances. Sharon seemed to accept the explanation, however, as she shook her head.

'He didn't say where he was going,' she said sadly.

'Did he ask for any directions?' Brodie asked.

'No. He only said he was doing some fishing over the next few days.'

'Fishing?'

'Apparently he owns a boat down at the harbor.'

She produced a map from under the counter. 'This is how you get to the marina.'

Brodie already had a pretty good idea of its location. She had spotted it on the way to the hotel. She thanked Sharon and hurried out of the premises with Dan close behind. She rang Agent Palmer immediately.

'That's great news,' the agent responded. 'We'll pick you up in five minutes.'

In less than five minutes their car appeared and they piled into the back seat of the vehicle.

'Sounds like you got luckier than us,' Palmer said. 'Chad succeeded in getting us into a fight.'

Sitting in the front seat, he turned around looking embarrassed.

'The guy said something about my hair,' he muttered. 'I said he should mind his own business.'

'You're incorrigible,' Brodie said.

'I'll second that,' Dan responded. 'Whatever it means.'

They arrived at the boat harbor within minutes. There seemed to be moorings for about five hundred vessels, all of them relatively small. Most of them were clearly leisure boats, though there were also a number of fishing trawlers.

Agent Palmer quickly located the harbor master's office. A man behind the desk recognized Wolff immediately.

'Sure,' he came through here. 'That's Joe Masterton. He owns a boat here.'

'Where is it?' Palmer asked.

'It's usually moored down at Row C,' he said. 'But I saw him take his boat out a little while ago.'

'Any idea where he would be headed?'

He shook his head. 'Could be anywhere.'

Palmer got the registration number of Wolff's vessel. 'We'll need a vessel. Where do I find one?'

The man referred them to a boat hire place. The grizzled man working behind the counter quickly hired them a small cabin cruiser. As soon as the man showed them to the vessel, Palmer was on her phone. After a couple of minutes she hung up and turned to the others.

'I think we might have a break,' she said. 'There is a report of a vessel leaving here less than an hour ago. It was heading out through Prince William Sound into a place called Jack Bay.'

'How did you find that out?' Brodie asked in amazement.

'We have satellites watching the entire planet,' Palmer said. 'Fortunately one of them was monitoring this area.'

They boarded their boat and Agent Palmer gently eased it away from the boat harbor before revving the speed up to maximum throttle. Brodie and the others grabbed a seat in the back of the cabin as they roared across the bay.

She wondered how Axel was going in Paris. She shivered. The weather was probably a lot warmer than in Alaska.

'Need warming up,' Chad suggested.

'No thanks.'

He looked annoyed. 'What do you see in that guy?'

'What guy?'

'Axel. He's such a dweeb.'

'He's a nice guy.' She shook her head. 'You should try it some time.'

Chad sighed. 'Don't take me the wrong way. I owe the guy my life, but he's not exactly Mr. Cool.'

'Have you looked at yourself lately?' Brodie asked.

'Sure,' he said. 'It's up to me to set a standard for others to follow.'

'You're delusional.'

'Sure.' He straightened his hair. 'But what a delusion.'

Brodie didn't say anything. She sat back and thought about the last few days. Already their time at Camp Sanctuary was fading away. She hoped she would never see Jeremiah Stead for as long as she lived. That maniac needed to be placed into a deep cell and the key thrown away. She thought about his son, Jason.

Jason Stead. He had been a good looking guy, but completely brainwashed by his father. She wondered what would happen to him now that he and the others had been taken into custody. She hoped there might be a chance of rehabilitation for him.

I could have been Brodie Stead, she thought. *Mrs. Brodie Stead.*

She rolled her eyes.

They rounded the headland and entered Jack bay. It was a wide, flat body of water, surrounded by forest on all sides. Fortunately it seemed quiet. Either fishermen didn't use this bay or they came here at other times during the day.

'Look,' Dan pointed.

A small boat lay moored at a ramshackle dock on one side. As they slowly drew close to it, Agent Palmer produced her gun. They peered past the vessel into the tree covered hillside. A small trail led away into the forest.

Brodie looked up the path and saw the back of a man heading up the hill. The man peered back at them and she saw his face clearly.

'It's him!' she said excitedly. 'It's Wolff!'

Chapter Thirty-Nine

We followed Wolff down the Parisian street. There were vacationers everywhere and fortunately they provided plenty of cover for us. While Agent Peterson, Ebony and I were able to successfully blend with the group, Ferdy stuck out like a sore thumb. He was able to easily keep up with us, but he could not really understand how to look like a regular tourist.

'Where do you think he's going?' Ebony asked.

'That's anyone's guess,' Agent Peterson said. 'The important thing is for us to take him down quietly and without fuss.'

I had already tried testing my powers and found them inoperative—again. Grinding my teeth in frustration, I thought of how easy this would be if my powers were working. I mentioned this as we wove our way through the crowds.

'Don't sweat it,' Peterson said. 'The scientists back at The Agency might have a solution. For the time being, just stay close.'

Wolff stopped when he reached an intersection. He hailed a cab.

'Damn,' the agent said. 'I didn't realize he was going to get a car.'

'Here's a cab,' Ebony said.

We flagged it over and piled in. Agent Peterson spoke quickly to the driver and pushed a bundle of money into his hand. The vehicle took off with a roar.

'I've promised to make it very worth his while if he can keep Wolff's cab in sight,' he said.

His phone rang and he answered it, keeping the other vehicle in sight at the same time. He muttered a few words before hanging up.

'That's strange,' he said. 'The other team has just reported in from Alaska.'

'And?' I asked.

'They told HQ that they had Wolff in sight.'

'That's impossible. He's in that cab ahead of us.'

'Is it possible that's not Wolff?'

'That's him,' Ebony said. 'I'd recognize him

anywhere. Even at a distance.'

The agent nodded thoughtfully. 'Okay. We'll play this as if he is Wolff. If anything changes we'll act accordingly.'

The taxi followed the other vehicle down the Parisian streets. At any other time I would have been excited to be heading through such a fantastic city, but I was too on edge to relax. The driver was good, though, and kept close to the other vehicle without arousing suspicion. After a few minutes we pulled into a tree lined street signposted as the Avenue de la Bourdonnais. Small apartment buildings and cafes enclosed both sides of it.

Through the side streets on our left we could see the Eiffel Tower. Finally the cab pulled over to the side of the road. Peterson told our driver to stop. We poured out of the vehicle and took refuge in a nearby tourist store while keeping Wolff under surveillance.

'Where's he going?' Ebony asked.

'I think I know where,' Peterson said. 'He might be meeting someone who can make adjustments to the virus.'

'What do you mean?' I asked.

'The virus is largely worthless right now,' Agent Peterson explained. 'It's so powerful no sane person would ever release it.'

'No sane person,' Ebony agreed, thinking of Jeremiah Stead and his group.

'But if Wolff can convince someone to manipulate the virus to make it less deadly or to target a specific ethnic group—'

'It's possible to do that?' I asked.

'It's possible,' Peterson confirmed. 'It would make the virus infinitely more valuable to blackmail world governments.'

'Blackmail,' Ferdy said. 'Meaning to extort money through the use of threats—'

'Thank you, Ferdy,' Agent Peterson said.

We watched as Wolff headed down one of the side streets.

'I think he's meeting someone at the Eiffel Tower,' Peterson continued.

'Why do it in such a busy location?' Ebony

asked.

'For his own protection,' Peterson said. 'The sort of people that Wolff deals with are as trustworthy as Wolff himself.'

We made our way across the thoroughfare toward the base of the Eiffel Tower. It was a grand structure made up of three levels. I had seen it on television and in magazines, but it was nothing compared to seeing it in person. As we headed along a passenger boulevard Peterson quickly told us about the tower.

'The first two levels can be accessed through either the elevator or stairs,' he said. 'The top level is via the elevators only.'

I looked up the length of the tower. I could see why.

I experimentally tried my powers as we reached the base of the tower. Much to my surprise I found they were working again—I was able to move a pile of leaves without effort.

Agent Peterson's eyes focused on us. 'I was thinking about leaving the three of you down here,' he said. 'I wasn't sure that your powers would help in this situation.'

'But surely—'

He nodded. 'I'll gladly accept your assistance.'

He went up to a pair of police officers and flashed some identification at them. He spoke to them, returning to us after a minute.

'I'm having the whole area closed down,' he said. 'We need to capture Wolff, but at all costs the vial must not be allowed to break. If it breaks—'

'It's game over,' I finished.

He nodded. Ebony looked scared, but determined. Even Ferdy looked solemn. I think at some level he understood that something serious was happening.

'My guess is he'll take the elevator to the top,' Peterson said. 'We'll start there. The whole base will be surrounded by the French police within minutes.'

We headed toward the elevators. We were lucky. Not many people were in line at that moment. Climbing into the elevator I looked at the vacationers around us. A husband and wife were arguing about the amount of time they could spend at the tower before they had to catch their flight. They were right about one thing.

Time was running out.

Chapter Forty

Brodie and the others disembarked from the boat and went racing up the trail.

'The vial must not be broken!' Agent Palmer yelled, hurrying ahead of them. 'Whatever happens, you must—'

A shot rang out and the agent spun around. Brodie and the others threw themselves to the ground. Palmer tried to get back up, but she had been hit in the shoulder. Blood began to pour profusely from the wound.

Brodie scrambled over to her. 'Are you okay?'

'Forget about me,' she grunted. 'You've got to stop Wolff. And whatever happens, don't break the vial.'

'We won't,' Brodie said. 'I promise.'

Brodie looked around. They needed some sort of shield.

'Dan,' she said. 'We need some cover.'

'Okay,' he said.

He knew he might be able to deflect bullets

from striking them, but he had to see them first. A shield was the safer option. He focused on the interior of the boat and within seconds they heard the screeching of metal. A piece of metal decking rose up over the boat and hovered before them.

'We'll come back to you,' Brodie promised Palmer.

'Don't worry about me,' she said. 'Just get the virus.'

They slowly made their way up the hill using the shield for cover. It was impossible to see Wolff ahead of them. The trail was fairly well used, but he could be hiding anywhere. Brodie felt quite nervous about moving up the track. This whole thing could be a trick. Wolff could hide in the forest and come out behind them.

Finally they reached a crest in the hill. Beyond it the trail continued down to a small bay. Another old dock jutted out into the water. It looked abandoned.

'I don't see Wolff,' Chad said. 'Maybe he didn't come this way.'

'It looks like the trail branches off over there,'

Brodie pointed.

They followed the turn. Ahead of them they heard a grinding sound. It was as if two rocks were moving against each other. Moving even more slowly they continued along to the trail.

'Look!' Dan yelled.

They spotted a pile of boulders over to their right. One of them was moving against the other.

'It's an opening to a cave!' Brodie yelled.

Chad flung out his hand and formed an icy barrier between the stones. They slowed, but did not stop completely.

'Wolff must have gone through there,' Brodie said. 'Quickly!'

They raced through the undergrowth. Chad's icy doorstop was threatening to shatter completely with each passing second. Dan leapt through with the hovering shield. Chad went next. Brodie jumped through at the last instant before the ice broke completely. She slammed into Chad and they went flying onto the ground.

She found herself on top of him.

He gave her a cheeky grin. 'I knew you liked me.'

She hit him in the chest. 'Like hell.'

They climbed to their feet and looked around. A tunnel had been built within the hill. It dipped down steeply into the earth. Florescent lighting lined the ceiling. Fortunately the tunnel ahead appeared fairly smooth on both sides; there were no alcoves where Wolff could be hiding.

A sound reverberated up the passageway.

'That sounds like water,' Chad said.

They headed down the incline. As the tunnel began to level out Brodie realized they were looking at a natural underground cave. A huge harbor lay before them. A wharf jutted out into the water.

Just as they reached the bottom, Dan noticed his shield wavering slightly in the air.

'What's—' he started.

The shield dipped and shuddered in the air before it fell to the ground.

'My powers,' he said. 'I couldn't keep—'

A voice came from the other side of the cave.

'Your powers are useless here, children.' Wolff stepped out from behind a boulder. 'Guns are the only power that matter here.'

He raised his weapon and opened fire.

Chapter Forty-One

The elevator reached the top of the Eiffel Tower and we stepped out into a crowded tourist space. The journey up the tower had been slow, but my heart rate had been rising with every second. I was afraid. So many things could go wrong. Wolff was an individual without morals. One of us could get killed.

Then there was the issue of the virus.

If the vial broke…

My heart thudded so hard in my chest I felt dizzy. The observation area was an enclosed platform with glass running around the exterior. People were moving in all directions. Tourists from every country and speaking every language were taking photos and roaming around the interior. A baby was crying. A school group of uniformed teenagers were making their way through the crowd.

Above the windows were photos comparing the height of the tower in relation to other tall structures around the world.

Paris lay outside.

'You kids know what Wolff looks like,' Peterson said. 'I'd prefer you let me take him down, but take him if you must. Just remember—'

'Don't break the vial,' Ebony said. 'I know.'

Ferdy looked around. 'There's the bad man.'

We all looked around. People were everywhere so it was impossible to see where Ferdy was looking. I realized it was quite cold on the observation deck. It took me a few seconds to realize that stairs led to an upper deck which opened onto an outside viewing platform.

'Was he going up the stairs?' I asked Ferdy.

'Stairs,' he said. 'A step is made up of a tread and a riser.'

That didn't help very much. We gently pushed our way through the crowd toward the stairs and cautiously ascended. We passed a room containing a statue of the designer, Gustave Eiffel. I barely glanced at it as I focused on trying to pick out Wolff in the crowd. We stepped outside onto the exterior platform. It was enclosed by a cage designed to stop people from either falling or jumping to their deaths.

Tourists were everywhere.

I slowly made my way around the exterior. A Japanese family got in my way so I navigated my way around them. Now a man was before me on one knee saying something to a blushing girl.

He was proposing.

I looked past them and at that instant saw Wolff come around a turn in the tower. His mouth fell open with surprise. I must have been the last person he expected to see. The last time I had seen him was on an island called Cayo Placetas where he was busily launching a nuclear weapon designed to destroy New York City.

Well, you never know who you'll run into on the Eiffel Tower.

He reached into his pocket and withdrew something. I formed a shield and screamed out at the same time.

'He's got a gun! He's got a gun!'

People started to move and yell in confusion. At the same moment, I realized it wasn't a gun in

Wolff's hand.

It was a hand grenade.

He pulled the pin and dropped the explosive onto the deck. He tried to push his way through the crowd, but there were too many people. I extended my arm and focused on forming a shield around the device. At first it worked. I started to form a barrier, a tight shield that—

No. Not now.

My powers failed.

No. Not now of all times. Not—

The grenade exploded.

Chapter Forty-Two

Bullets were flying everywhere. Fortunately a boulder lay to one side and Brodie dragged Chad and Dan behind it as Wolff opened fire. The sound of ricocheting ammunition sounded all around them.

She peered over the top of the stone.

'You children should get a refund on your powers,' Wolff taunted. 'They are too easily defeated through the use of zeno emitters.'

Tell me something I don't know, Brodie thought. *Except my powers are a little different to the others.*

She had already worked out Wolff's plan. The jetty seemed to meet another structure protruding from the water. A submarine. Once Wolff was in the craft he would escape. Despite her powers being zapped by the zeno rays, she still had fighting ability she had inherited from her previous life. She had no idea where it came from. She only knew she innately understood half a dozen martial arts.

Wolff fired two more shots. His clip was

empty. Brodie broke from cover and charged across the cave floor. She was slower than usual. Under normal circumstances she was three times the speed of a highly trained athlete. Now she did not have that advantage.

She would have to survive without it.

Wolff saw her coming. His eyes opened in wonder. Obviously he had not expected one of these children to make a suicidal run across the floor. At the same time Brodie saw him glance at the submarine.

He raced up the length of the dock. By the time Brodie reached the start of the wooden structure, he had stepped onto the metal conning tower of the submarine. He gave her a sneering grin and stepped on to the top of the ladder.

That's when it happened.

When Brodie thought about it later, when she analyzed those seconds in her mind one frame at a time, she realized that Wolff did not step properly onto the top rung of the ladder. His leg twisted beneath him.

He slipped.

He fell.

Brodie put on more speed and reached the sub within seconds. She looked down the length of the ladder. Wolff lay on the floor below. His leg was twisted at a crazy angle beneath him. Broken. He pulled a vial of liquid from his pocket and stared at it in horror.

It had a crack in it.

Brodie grabbed the top hatch of the submarine and slammed it down. She spun the locking mechanism around furiously until it was sealed as tightly at it would go. All the while she heard Wolff screaming from within the submarine.

Only at the end, when the virus had fully taken effect, did his screaming end.

Chapter Forty-Three

The carnage was immediate and devastating.

The blast pushed me backwards. I felt my eyes surge back into their sockets as the detonation of the grenade impacted against me. Slamming into a group of tourists behind me, I heard the explosion and after that everything faded to silence.

I could see, but I could not make sense of what I saw. The explosion had reduced everything to reverberating roar in my ears. Images like frames of a movie came to me. Disjointed. Piecemeal.

Slowly I made sense of the carnage.

The grenade had torn away part of the metal plating from the deck of the Eiffel Tower. It had destroyed a wide section of the barrier. People and blood and body parts lay everywhere.

Somehow, incredibly, Wolff was still on his feet. Or perhaps foot was a better description. One of his legs was mostly gone. One of his arms was missing completely. He reached into his pocket.

The vial was in his hand. He took a single

staggering step forward before falling face first onto the deck. Whatever he intended to do with the vial was unclear. It bounced from his hand across the deck. I could not hear anything. I certainly could not hear Ebony's scream as she appeared from nowhere and threw herself after it.

As the vial rolled off the deck, Ebony reached after it, but she was overbalanced. The entire top half of her body slid over the edge as she desperately grabbed for the vial. Struggling to my feet, I started toward her. My entire body hurt. It would not obey my commands.

Move!

Somehow, my body moved forward.

Ebony lay precariously unbalanced over the side of the shattered deck. She tried reaching back to grab something to stop her momentum, but her hands grasped only air.

She started to slide over.

I threw myself at her. My hand reached for her and closed around her belt. I had her. Solid. Nothing would make me release her.

Except now I was sliding after her. My other hand desperately tried to grasp the deck, but it was smooth metal. I tried to focus on my powers, but my brain was too addled to make anything work.

Her entire body slid over the edge. I reached out desperately for help.

This was it.

The end of everything.

No, please don't let it—

A hand sprang out of nowhere. A small hand. It grasped my hand and pulled me away from the edge, almost dislocating my arm from its socket. I dragged Ebony up from over the side onto the deck. In her hand lay the vial with the deadly blue liquid safely contained within.

We lay there panting and crying with relief as Ferdy grabbed the both of us close to him.

I could not hear his words because I was still shell shocked by the blast of the grenade, but I could read his lips.

'Ferdy's friends,' he was saying. 'Ferdy's friends.'

'That's right,' I said, although I could not hear myself speak. 'Ferdy's friends.'

Chapter Forty-Four

'Okay,' Chad said. 'I've got about a million questions, but let me just start with one.'

'I think I can guess what it is,' Agent Peterson said. 'How was it possible for Wolff to be in two places at once?'

We were seated on the fourth floor of the building that made up part of the Las Vegas branch of The Agency. Three days had passed since the explosion on the top of the Eiffel Tower. There had been mourning all over the world for the six people killed and the dozens injured during the blast.

A terrorist organization had taken claim for the blast. That had struck me as ridiculous. Clearly Wolff had acted alone, but obviously some other group was seizing the chance to increase exposure for their own organization.

There are some sick people in this world. Who would want to be associated with such an evil event?

Have it your own way, I thought. *Just as long as the world is safe.*

We had come close to failing. Too close. The vial in Alaska had actually broken open. If it weren't for Brodie's quick thinking the whole planet would have ended up a much quieter place. Engineers were removing the submarine from its underground enclosure and delivering it to a secret facility. There, it would be destroyed in an underground furnace constructed to reduce anything to atoms.

We had saved the day, but it did not feel like a victory. Rather it felt more like delaying the inevitable.

Agent Palmer was recuperating in hospital. She was expected to make a full recovery. The rest of us were in various stages of recuperation. I had been severely stunned by the blast. Chad still had his wounds from our time in Yodak Jail. He was the kind of guy who preferred to hide his pain.

A day after we returned, I found a block of my favorite chocolate sitting on my bed. At first I thought Brodie had brought it for me, but it turned out to be Chad. When I asked him about it he wouldn't even look at me.

'It's just to say thanks,' he said, staring at the floor. 'Don't think we're BFF's now.'

'I wouldn't dream of it,' I replied.

'But…thanks,' he said.

I thought of that terrible Yodak Jail and everyone else suffering in North Korea and places like that where freedom was a luxury that most people did not enjoy.

'That's okay,' I held out my hand to shake.

He looked at the hand, shook his head and laughed. 'Dweeb.'

Chad. Who can work him out?

Agent Peterson's voice broke into my reverie. 'We believe Wolff is a type of mod,' he said. 'Checking DNA samples he left at both locations, we were able to ascertain that both versions of him were more than twins. They were actually the same person.'

'So his power is…' Ebony's voice trailed off.

'We think he has the ability to copy himself,' Peterson said. 'We have no idea how many versions of him are running around.'

I shook my head in amazement. 'One version of him is bad enough. Let's hope they're all finally gone.'

'Identical twins occur in about three of every thousand births,' Ferdy said.

'And talking about gone,' Chad said. 'I think it's time we went on our merry way.'

Peterson shook his head. 'You boys made a promise to The Agency that you would remain as part of the organization. What about that promise?'

'We were being blackmailed at the time,' Chad said firmly. 'By The Agency. We didn't have a choice in the matter.'

The agent put up a hand. 'Before you do anything too hasty, I think there's something you should know.'

'What?' three of us asked simultaneously.

And laughed.

'The Secretary General of the United Nations, Sunil Verma, made a speech to General Assembly about an hour ago.' Peterson paused. 'He broke the news to the member states and indeed the entire world's population that there are people on Earth who have been modified. This means we're now living in a new age. Just as the explosion of the atomic bomb heralded the beginning of the nuclear age, we're now living in an era where mods will be part of our everyday lives.

'You and people like you will be known to the world from this day forward. If you want to be.'

No-one seemed to know what to say. Even Chad looked stuck for words.

Agent Peterson continued. 'There have already been sightings of people exhibiting unusual powers. People in Russia filmed a man flying over the city less than an hour after the announcement.'

'So we're...out of the closet?' Ebony asked and blushed.

'If you want to be.' Agent Peterson sat down at the table. 'These are early days yet and you all have a long way to go. You all need to train yourselves and learn to use your powers. The world needs modified humans now more than ever.'

'You mean there's going to be factories

churning out modified people like us?' Chad stammered.

'Not at all,' Peterson said. 'Although there have been mods for centuries it will still be illegal to experiment with the human genome. Of course, that will not stop some nations from still doing so.'

'It certainly didn't stop The Agency,' Brodie said. 'And what about the Bakari?'

She was referring to the aliens who had been working with The Agency for centuries to prepare mankind for the intergalactic era.

'People still don't know about The Agency,' Peterson said. 'Nor do they know about The Bakari. We intend to keep it that way.'

'So we could leave here and become circus performers if we want,' Dan said. 'Cool.'

'Circuses are fun,' Ferdy said. 'Ferdy can be a lion tamer.'

Peterson raised an eyebrow. 'If you want. But you may be interested to know that a man broke into a bank in Malaysia a short time ago. Witnesses claim he used some sort of power from his eyes to melt the doors of the vault.'

'So we can be super villains?' Chad asked. 'Cool.'

I hoped he wasn't serious. I was thinking about my own powers. In the last few days I had tried to use them a number of times and nothing had happened. I had not even been able to raise a sheet of paper with my mind. I had told Brodie about my dilemma and she told me to just give it time.

What if my powers never returned?

It was not losing my powers that bothered me. It was losing the only family I knew. How could I be part of a superhero team when I had no powers?

'I know a great injustice was done to you all,' Agent Peterson continued. 'I know you are the victims of an illegal experiment, but I would like to ask you to stay on. As a team, working together, you can accomplish great things.' He looked at each of us in turn. 'What do you say?'

It was several minutes before anyone spoke.

Epilog

The waves raced up and down the beach. A man and his daughter chased them. The man was middle aged. His daughter was seven years old. They laughed and screamed with delight as they dared the waters of the Atlantic to catch their feet.

Finally the man noticed the sun cresting the horizon and the air growing colder with every passing minute. Soon it would be night. They gathered their things together and walked toward the dunes.

Within minutes the beach lay deserted and silent.

An arm reached out from the water. The head of a man followed. Then shoulders. After a minute, a naked man ascended the beach and marched resolutely up the sand. He sheltered in an alcove away from the cold night air.

He shivered, wrapping his arms around himself.

Watching the waves, he saw a movement in the waves. A man's head appeared. His naked body followed. The newcomer walked from the water, peered across the darkening beach and joined his companion.

They sat side by side on the sand in the gathering darkness.

Time to start again, Solomon Wolff thought.

A Few Final Words

I hope you enjoyed reading The Doomsday Device. It is the second book in the Teen Superheroes series. There are many more to enjoy! The other books are:

Diary of a Teenage Superhero (Book 1)

The Battle for Earth (Book 3)

The Twisted Future (Book 4)

Terminal Fear (Book 5)

I love hearing from my readers. You can contact me at darrellpitt@gmail.com

Thanks again and happy reading!

Darrell

Y Pitt Darrell v.2
Pitt, Darrell
The doomsday device Book two

CPSIA information can be obtained
at www.ICGtesting.com
Printed in the USA
LVOW03s1453140617
538110LV00010B/517/P

9 781516 952427